The Androgyne Papyrus

Book Two

THE ANDROGYNE PAPYRUS

Book Two

Robert Hodgson, Jr.

CAHABA PRESS

Eureka Springs
Arkansas
USA

Cahaba Press
483 CR 231
Eureka Springs, AR 72631
cahabapublishing.com

Copyright © 2022

Robert Hodgson, Jr.
All Rights Reserved

Cover Design by Jenny McGee
Copyright cover image © 2022 Jenny McGee
See more of Jenny's work at artistjennymcgee.com
Created with Vellum.

ISBN: 9798844602283

For Mary Timothy Downs Hodgson

I have to begin with a few words about androgyny.

Nora Ephron, "A Few Words about Breasts"

Preface

Summary of Book One

It's the summer of 1967. The Beatles release Sgt. Pepper's Lonely Hearts Club Band. A gallon of gas runs 33 cents. Troop strength in Vietnam surges to more than a half a million soldiers. Race riots in Cleveland, Newark, Detroit, and Milwaukee scorch America's inner cities. Radical feminism shoots to the forefront of the Women's Movement. The Catholic Church retrenches after largely turning away from Pope John XXIII's aggiornamento "modernization" of the Catholic Church. Among the reforms that survived was a renewed effort to confront sexual abuse of children by clergy.

Book One

Against this backdrop, Marquette Bible scholar Tom Weathering and his partner Chiara O'Keeffe (and mother of their daughter Faith) turn into a detective couple, a 1960s version of Nick and Nora Charles. Matching wits with violent operatives of the Sodality, the intelligence arm of the Vatican Bank, they set out to find the Androgyne Papyrus, the original Greek copy of Apostle Paul's lost Letter to the Laodiceans. The Letter, known only from later translations, makes the resounding claim that in Christ there is no male nor female. The upshot of this view is equally staggering: women have an equal role to play in the leadership of the Church. Despite the savage cunning of Sodality agents, Tom and Chiara locate the Papyrus only to have it slip from their grasp. Threats, assaults, and finally a bombing force the couple to relocate to Göttingen University in Germany.

Chapter One

Theology Professor Walther Zimmer clomped over the floor of his office toward his desk. The knee-hinge of his birchwood prosthetic ticked like a Swiss clock. With each footfall the hardwood gave back a slap-smack that ground on his nerves. The sound brought up hard memories from his years in a Russian gulag, above all the cruel thump of a guard's baton on his back.

Zimmer lifted up a walnut picture frame from his desk. His hand quivered. A faded black and white photograph crinkled against a cover glass. Zimmer blew out a long, slow breath. He scanned the line of reed-thin German POWs, grinning ghoulishly into a camera. The sharp outlines of caved-in faces, leering at a journalist through barbed-wire fencing, painted a graffito of human misery.

Even now, so many years later, Zimmer felt his flesh creep at the mud and excrement that besmirched their faces and clothing. He ran a finger over the tattered greatcoats, the rotting boots, the moth-eaten scarves. Even now he could taste the weedy mold on the black bread they'd earned for posing.

Zimmer's finger traced the faces of Wilhelm with his big ears and Dabelstein with his forced smile. He winced as he studied the face of the ragged Orthodox priest in the middle of their line who clung to Wilhelm's arm. The old man had set off their hunt for the Apostle Paul's lost Letter to the Laodiceans that Tom Weathering dubbed the Androgyne Papyrus. How long ago that seemed. A lifetime of lifetimes.

Zimmer turned to face the office window behind his desk to clear his head. A creeping sinus headache warned of heavy weather from the North Sea. When a gust of wind slung ice pellets against the glass, he jerked back. A letter from his former student, J. Barriston Gordon, now professor of theology at Marquette University in Milwaukee, slipped from his hand.

With an audible groan Zimmer stooped to pick up the envelope. God, he hated to cave into old age. Especially early old age brought on by ten cruel years in the gulag.

He reread the two-pages, though it was a stretch to call the scribbled sheets a letter. The text was a screed of jerking and crabbing phrases whose thoughts danced all over the page. Gordon blamed catastrophes around the world on the Sodality, the Vatican Bank's secret department of heresy hunters. He fumed about riots in midtown Manhattan, Cairo, and Jerusalem. In each city Sodality operatives had tricked Jews, Christians, and Muslims into open conflict with each other over the lost letter and its sensational claims about Jesus Christ the androgyne.

The final paragraphs brought personal news. A vicious

beating had sent Gordon into the hospital. A church bombing in Milwaukee brought death and injury to a small multitude. Mercifully, Tom, Chiara, and Faith survived the blast, though shaken and burned. Sona Routanian, the Armenian graduate student who'd arranged for the *Panarion* to come to Marquette, had disappeared, along with her family.

Zimmer stuffed the letter into his jacket pocket. Slivers of ice tailed down his spine. The writer was not the student he knew ten years back for a low-key, clearheaded, and scholarly fellow. So bright and stable in fact that, two years earlier, Zimmer had entrusted to him photographs of the envelope pages with their Armenian text.

Zimmer read the final lines of Gordon's letter, pushing the palm of one hand against his cheek. He took comfort in the brighter news he found there. Tom Weathering and his family had slipped safely out of Milwaukee and left for Göttingen, several months earlier than planned. They were in fact due to visit his office that morning.

The news of the Americans' early arrival hadn't daunted Zimmer. He'd easily found a room for them at the Hotel Gebhards next to the train station. And Frau Wilhelm, Martin's widow, had promised a cozy apartment. The good news notwithstanding, Zimmer shuddered at a dark thought. How long before the Sodality tracked down the young couple in Göttingen?

Zimmer paced the floor again, his mind sidetracking to Frau Wilhelm and her children and how they'd dealt with the loss of a husband and father. The police had ruled Wilhelm's plunge from a third-floor library window a suicide. Zimmer knew better. Martin would never defenestrate himself. No, the Sodality had staged the death to look like a suicide. Zimmer turned to his window again, gazing across the wintery, elm-fringed square. Despite the ice storm he could make out the library balcony from which Wilhelm fell. It was hard to look at. Most days he kept the blinds closed.

The Biedermeier clock on the wall chimed 10 a.m. Damnation! The Americans were due any minute. Zimmer walked to a threadbare sofa that his wife salvaged from their home in Dresden when the British firebombed the city. Above the couch he'd hung a childlike painting of colorful circles and squares by Paul Klee, his father's colleague at the German Bauhaus in Berlin. Scant pickings, his wife liked to say, from a once comfortable life before the war.

Zimmer reached under a cushion for his Pervitin tablets and bottle of schnapps. Two tablets went down in a gurgling swallow, sticking for a moment in his throat. Coughing, he sat down on the sofa.

He closed his eyes. Yesterday his wife and his physician called him bullheaded for turning down a newer, aluminum prosthetic. Covered by insurance, they said. New device every three years. Noiseless. The old warrior in him shot back: he and Old Henry belonged together like a sausage and its skin. A clever Cossack doctor in the gulag saved his life by fashioning the shank in exchange for a pack of cigarettes. Friends did not throw away friends. He chuckled, recalling the exchange of helpless looks between his wife and his doctor.

As the tablets buffered his pain and cleared his head, he rifled through his memory of Gordon's earlier letters. They'd fairly run with praise for Tom and Chiara. The boy—that was Gordon's term—showed fine instincts as a researcher. He was methodical and analytic. Easy-going but ardent at the right moment. The girl—also Gordon's word—was an Irish-Italian spitfire with a mind and intellect of her own. There was a daughter, Faith: two, adept at puzzles, already verbal. Dear God! Zimmer gasped. It dawned on him that he'd taken on a whole family.

A gentle tap on his office door brought Zimmer to his feet. "Come in, please," he said. He heaved himself up from the sofa and waved his guests into the office. "Ha! So, we meet at last. Come in, come in, Herr Weathering, Frau O'Keeffe. Welcome to Göttingen." He lit the room up with a good, honest smile warm with delight.

Zimmer took their coats and seated his guests on two chairs in front of his desk. Running an eye over the couple's clothes, he wondered if they knew about northern European winters. Tom clearly didn't. He'd dressed casually in brown chinois slacks, a wooly cardigan, and a light anorak. His toes stuck out from a pair of summer sandals.

Chiara looked better outfitted in a turtleneck sweater and a pleated wool skirt over cable-knit tights. She bristled with warmth and energy, and he felt his own body heat notch up. He guessed their age at mid-twenties, about the age of the grandchildren he and his wife might have had, if Russian captivity hadn't sent him home a damage man. He swallowed a little bubble of regret.

"Welcome to Göttingen," Zimmer said. "And apologies for my cluttered office." He swung an arm in the direction of bookshelves, credenzas, and a massive oak table. Each looked on the verge of collapse under the weight of boxes of books and shards. "A little tidying up to do yet," he said apologetically, trying to hide the remains of a bratwurst and potato-salad meal under a folder.

"Thank you, sir," Tom said. "Nice to meet you."

"Where's the child?"

"With a babysitter at the hotel," Chiara said.

"The trip across...how was it?"

"Tiring," Tom said. "And humdrum. I think our cover as tourists held. At least we don't think anyone shadowed us *en route*. At least we hope so."

Zimmer grunted. The mention of a shadow set off a nagging anxiety. One of Gordon's letters warned that the Sodality had stationed several people in Milwaukee. He looked into Chiara's face then into Tom's. He waited for some sign of trouble to come up behind their eyes. "You're sure?" Zimmer said, forcing himself to sound curious rather than alarmed.

"Umm, I think so," Tom said."

"That's good," Zimmer said with a measured voice, "Now that you're here we'll want to keep our business to ourselves."

"Promise," the two Americans said.

Zimmer nodded. The young couple had spine. Now he had to be sure they knew how to spot danger. He'd pay close attention to them over the next weeks. "Look," he said, "there's a letter from Gordon that we need to talk about."

Surprise flared in Tom and Chiara's eyes. They exchanged glances. "Letter?" Chiara said. "We didn't expect to hear from Gordon until after the New Year."

"I'm afraid there's hard news from Milwaukee." He slipped Gordon's letter from under a desk blotter. "Professor Gordon is in the hospital recovering from a blow to his skull with a candlestick. And the police haven't located your friend Sona Routanian and her children. As you know she fled the city with her family."

Zimmer hated moments like this. The awful news spurted like blood from an artery. He was a scholar not a counselor. Well, he was in the thick of it now.

"No!" Chiara cried, her voice rasping with shock. She seized Tom's hand.

"We haven't had any updates since leaving Milwaukee," Tom said. "Gordon told us not to leave a forwarding address…"

Zimmer held out the letter to Tom. "In case you want to read it yourselves. I'll do anything to help you." He stood up from his desk. "Old Henry's pinching me." He tapped on his prosthetic. He didn't know what else to do. He felt helpless in the moment and walked across the office toward the sofa. He glanced over his shoulder and saw Tom and Chiara motionless in a stunned huddle. A piercing wail split the office silence as Chiara threw her head back and screamed "Not Sona and her children. No, no, no." Tom wrapped an arm around her shoulder, the letter fluttered to the floor.

7

Zimmer turned back to his desk. He gripped Tom and Chiara's shoulders with his hands. "I know there's nothing I can say to make the pain go away. And I understand if you have second thoughts about the Project." Two defiant faces looked up at him, and he knew right away he'd misjudged their pluck. They were young and brazen enough to discount danger and feel untouchable. "I'm glad you want to stay. Gordon would want that. Look, I can give you a little balm for your hurt. There's good news from my friend, Frau Wilhelm."

"Thanks," Chiara said. "We feel a little short on good news just now."

"She found a cozy apartment behind her house. You're expected tomorrow at 4:30 p.m. for tea. Most likely she'll have a houseful of family."

Chiara said, "Thanks for reaching out to Frau Wilhelm. I have a feeling she'll be more than a kind neighbor."

"I think so," Zimmer said. "She'll see to your needs in ways that I cannot. Just remember that the family is still dealing with the loss of a husband and father. And conflicted, too. The children have sided with the coroner and the police and accepted a verdict of suicide. Frau Wilhelm—not so much. I think she may ask you both to dig deeper into the matter. Be sure to ask for the journals and notes Professor Wilhelm left behind. There's more to his death than meets the eye."

Chapter Two

Göttingen, December 1966

Zimmer reached for the walnut picture frame on his desk and offered it to Tom, who squared the photo in his hands, showing it to Chiara.

Chiara said, "You three were all close?"

"Yes. Wilhelm, Dabelstein, and I studied theology together at Tübingen," Zimmer said, his finger hovering over each figure. "Then the Russian front and gulag. He chuckled at a memory. "The Russians took us for geologists. Worked out OK. At university we'd learned archeology and had a notion of digging."

"You must've suffered horribly," Chiara said.

"Well, we got into some tight places with the Russians," Zimmer said. "After the battle of Vlosk, a Russian officer shot all the men in our squad. He ran out of bullets when he came to Dabelstein, Wilhelm, and me. After that brush with death, we three newly-minted geologists fought to keep each other alive for a better day. Nothing else mattered."

Despite their brave faces, the news from home had shaken the young couple. He was tempted to offer them his

Pervitin tablets. No, that was reckless. Best talk about the Project right away. Keep their minds busy and focused on making a new life for themselves. Not for nothing did we German professors call ourselves doctor-fathers.

"Look," Zimmer said with a loud handclap that started his visitors. "Next month I lecture before the Göttingen Academy of Science."

"What's the topic?" Chiara asked.

"Will the Real Jesus Please Stand up?" Zimmer said, breaking into a wide smile.

"OK, you got my attention," Tom said. "Tell us more."

"Well," Zimmer said, "by itself the Laodicean Letter and its androgyne Jesus can hardly offset two-millennia of male domination and predation in the Catholic Church. It needs the help of other long-forgotten versions of Jesus, even the ones the Church branded as off-beat and heretical."

"Ah, right," Tom said. "To show that in the early church several views of Jesus held the field. I've read some of the quirky stuff in the earlier parts of Epiphanius's book of heresies. Writings on Jesus the ray of light, or Jesus the god in human disguise."

"Yes and No," Zimmer said. "Epiphanius gathered up theological concepts and theories. I mean something else more concrete. My lecture shows cultural renderings of Jesus--drawings, images, forgotten and sidelined Christian art and artifacts."

"Yikes," Chiara said, "You've whetted our appetites. Go on."

"Well, first of all," Zimmer said, "I'd like you both to

attend as my special guests. What do you think?"

"Of course," Chiara said. "We'd love to. But we don't have any formal dress."

"I'll take care of that," Zimmer said. "Meanwhile, here's the big idea I'm putting in the lecture." Tom and Chiara leaned forward. "Ordinary Christians showed their day-to-day faith in Jesus by creating art and artifacts. Theologians and scholars used academic theology to illustrate faith."

"Wow, that's rad," Tom said. "The Jesus of culture side-by-side with the Jesus of theology."

"An image or artifact is worth a thousand words," Chiara said.

"Excellent," Zimmer said. "Let's look at a preview of the lecture." He called his assistant, Lisle, on his desk intercom. "Please come in and set up a projector and screen. We'll want coffee and cookies, too please." He motioned to Tom to pull the drapes. "Lisle will load the slides for us."

The first slide flashed on the screen: a childlike Jesus wearing a tunic, dressed as a shepherd. "One of the earliest images of Jesus in European culture," Zimmer said. "Rome. Third-century A.D. Catacomb of Callixtus."

"My God," Chiara said. "That Jesus is just a kid. How'd we ever get from there to Jesus the tall, blue-eyed, bearded Swede?"

The projector clicked and brought up a slide that showed Jesus as a nude child perched in a rippling pool of clear water. "Arian Baptistry. Sixth-century A.D. Ravenna," Zimmer said. The next image added a bearded, adult Jesus to the series. "Encaustic on panel. Called the Christ Pantokrator, the All-Powerful Christ. Fifth century A.D. Monastery of St. Catherine in the Sinai."

"So," Tom said, scribbling some notes on a sheaf of paper, "it took the Church nearly six hundred years to grow Jesus from an infant into a bearded adult. Wow!"

"Indeed," Zimmer said. "Next image please, Lisle."

A thin Negroid figure appeared on the screen. "That's the black Jesus of the Ethiopian Coptic Church of Africa. Goes back to the second, possibly even the first-century AD," Zimmer said, reaching for a cookie and dipping it in his coffee. "Jump ahead," he told his assistant, "to the last three images.

"Wait," Chiara said to Tom. "Our friend Joseph was so proud of the black figure of Saint Bonaventure at his church."

"Righto," Tom said. "Not so strange if Ethiopian Christians had their black Jesus nearly two-thousand years ago."

The projector whirled through dozens of slides before a starkly outlined, chocolate-faced figure with thick dreadlocks filled the screen. "The Jamaican Rastafarian Jesus," Zimmer said.

An image of a feathered serpent slithered across the screen. "That's Quetzalcoatl, the Mayan God," Zimmer said. "Still popular among some Mayan Christians who picture Jesus as a feathered serpent who died and was resurrected."

The last slide—the crucified Christ of the Kongo people—clicked into the chamber. A carved statue with bulging, oval eyes and two feet blended into one five-toed foot spread across the screen.

"Gosh," Chiara said, vaulting out of her chair for a closer look. "That's frightening."

"So, what do you think?" Zimmer asked. Will my slides poke my peers at the Academy and get them to think about the historical Jesus differently?"

"Think so," Tom said.

"With all due respect, sir," Chiara said, "there's something missing. Don't we need a slide of an androgyne Jesus to complete the story?"

"Yes, of course," Zimmer said with a head slap. "Hmm. Chiara has a point. Trouble is that artifacts and images of an androgyne Jesus, if there were any, didn't survive the iconoclasts and heresy hunters. Still, one or two slides of Greek and Roman androgynes in the Greco-Roman style might fill the gap."

"It would show that Christian artisans," Tom said, "had a model for the androgyne Jesus."

Zimmer glanced at the wall clock. "Yikes, I've got to meet my wife for lunch. Before you go, may I ask you something about one of Gordon's letters?"

"Of course," Tom said, "What's up?"

"He wrote that at Marquette you took a close look at the *Panarion*."

"Yes, it was breathtaking," Tom said.

"Gordon said you found something puzzling about the codex."

"Right," Tom said. "Gordon and I measured the thickness of those last three leaves or folios, the ones with

13

the Armenian version of the Letter to the Laodiceans. We had a hunch those leaves might be envelope pages that held fragments of the original Greek text of the Letter. What we came to call the Androgyne Papyrus. Trouble was we didn't have a caliper, only a ruler to get an exact measurement of thickness. But to the touch those pages sure seemed thicker than all that went before. By twice as much we guessed."

Zimmer ran a hand over his head. The mention of Venice made him feel his age and disability. "Well," he said, "I hate to tell you weary travelers that it's no longer if but when."

Chiara came to life. "You mean return to Venice? Count us in. As soon as we're settled into the apartment, we're good to go."

Tom said, "Gordon told us about the first time you showed him the photocopies of those last three folios. You said to him 'They traveled a long way to you and me. Treat them with reverence. A time will come for them to take their place in history'."

Zimmer said, "That time has come. And good luck with your visit to Frau Wilhelm. As soon as you're settled in, we'll book your train for Venice."

Chapter Three

City tram Number 5 clanged its bell as it braked at the foot of a steep hill. Chiara stepped out of a heated carriage onto slippery cobblestones. Tom followed, clasping Faith by the hand. As the sliding door snapped shut, snow whipped against their faces and crunched under their boots. Chiara threw Tom a strained look. It was time to meet their host family, the Wilhelms. She had a thousand questions. And didn't know where to start.

Alone on the street, they shivered, stamped their feet, and flipped coat collars up. Chiara gave Faith's wooly neck scarf an extra turn. "Hold Mama's hand, darling," she said. "The path is slippery." She glanced at the daffodil bouquet in Tom's hand. A gift for Frau Wilhelm, Tom had nearly crushed it. "Hold the flowers bud-side down," she said.

"Oops, sorry. Bummer," Tom said, tipping the bouquet over. "Got ruffled looking around for our landmark. OK. There it is, the Greek restaurant on the right." His words left his mouth in a vapor trail. He sniffed the air. "I'm guessing garlic roasted lamb? My stomach's grumbling."

"Me, too, Papa," Faith said.

"Have a little patience," Chiara begged. "I'm sure Frau Wilhelm will put a lovely tea together." She pointed toward a street sign. "This is Nonnenstieg. Follow me. It's a climb," she said. Hands clasped, they worked their way through a neighborhood of cozy bungalows set back from a cobblestone walk. Woodsy, resinous evergreens scented the walkway and small yards and brushed against their faces. "Number 60 must be near the top, on the left."

Near the crown of the hill, Chiara's mind pinwheeled back in time. She turned to look at the tracks they'd stamped on the sidewalk. Two large sets of boot prints, like protective rails, bracketed one small set. In an hour the wind would blow their footfalls away, time would erase the record of their trek. Would time also cover up the lingering sadness and sorrow they'd carried with them to Germany? She thought of Sona Routanian gone missing with her family. Of Father Grapiano and Precious Dilbarton, both dead and buried after the church bombing; of Professor Gordon, struggling for his life in a hospital. For an instant she craved their makeshift but cozy apartment in Milwaukee and her rowdy, needy class of inner-city schoolchildren.

Her foot slipped on the ice and Tom caught her arm.

"Thanks, honey, I nearly went down." Come on, girl, pay attention to the moment at hand. She wished she'd told Tom how much the prospect of visiting the Wilhelm family rattled her. Was it too soon after the professor's suicide? What ghosts lurked between those walls? Truth was she felt awkward asking Frau Wilhelm for help. The poor woman

16

had borne troubles enough without taking on the care of an itinerant family.

What a turnaround from the easy-going, charmed life of their first year together. They'd felt whole, inspired, able to lark and prank and laugh off every setback. In their Milwaukee apartment, she'd learned how to cook meals. He knew recipes by heart. One evening she'd watched him add cans of mushrooms and chipped beef to a package of macaroni and cheese.

"That's not part of the instructions," she said, waving the box under his nose. "You're not allowed to do that, are you?" He said yes, and she wagged her head as if he had just discovered radium.

The Project had ground them both down, and now for days on end she found herself vulnerable and unmoored, jumping at shadows. She no longer wondered if events might overtake them. It was when. Not so many weeks ago they'd joked about playing a detective family. A 1960s version of Dashiell Hammett's Nick and Nora Charles. Hustling for clues. Dodging mysterious evildoers. Raising a child. Not anymore. The game had turned into a hunt, and they were now the prey.

Stop this she told herself. They'd made choices. Now, clear heads and stout hearts were the order of the day. True, the news from Milwaukee had knocked them down. But in Professor Zimmer and Frau Wilhelm they'd found safety and hope and a way forward. Tom had a fresh start on the Project, the family had a safe apartment.

"So, here we are," Chiara said, pulling up at *Nonnenstieg* 60, a two-story bungalow with a red tile roof.

She pointed at the eyebrow dormers that winked down on them. "House looks like an owl," she told Faith. "Just right for the home of an academic." She caught herself. A dead academic.

They hiked up flagstone steps to the front door. It was ajar. A bell button hung loosely on two wires. Chiara pressed twice before a figure in trousers and undershirt opened the door and peered nearsightedly at her. The scent of cinnamon and buttery sugar mixed with the din of pots from a kitchen wafted around the man in the doorframe.

A gob of shaving lather with a smear of blood clung to the right side of his face. A straightedge razor blade glinted dangerously in one hand. Chiara took a step back. The man looked flurried. His eyes blinked as if unused to daylight. She peeked around the figure into a dim hallway. At the other end of the corridor she saw a living room. Someone played a piano and did it awfully well.

"Bloody doorbell," the man said, staunching his bleeding cheek with a handkerchief. "Goes off every time I try to shave."

Chiara caught the title of a slender volume under the man's other arm. *Collected Works of John Milton.* "Dangerous that," Chiara said, "reading poetry while shaving. Iambic pentameters cut something fierce." She smiled at the man who cocked his head, quizzically. Maybe he hadn't settled on talking with strangers.

The man fumbled absently in a pant pocket and found a pair of glasses. "Gosh," he said, sticking out a hand. "Sorry. Caught me by surprise. You must be the Americans Mutti invited. I'm Phil, her son-in-law. I'm American, too.

18

From Phoenix. Married to Anna. We're spending the Christmas holidays. You're her first visitors in months."

"I'm Chiara. This is Tom. And the little one is Faith." The man ruffled the child's hair with a brush of his hand.

"Pleased to meet you. Come in, come in. Let me have your coats."

A woman's voice called through a door off the hallway. "Who's here, Phil?"

"Ah, that would be Anna. She's in the kitchen," he said. "Anna, come meet our guests."

"In a minute. My cookies are burning."

"Smells scrumptious," Chiara said.

"Gingersnaps. Professor Wilhelm's favorite. Used to be, I mean."

"Mine, too," Tom said. Faith sniffed and made a rabbit nose at a spicy wave drifting past. A moment later, she darted for the kitchen door. "Faith, come back here," Chiara said, reaching for Faith's coattail.

"The little girl is fine," Phil said. "Anna will warm some milk and let her lick the cookie bowl."

"She loves to do that," Chiara said. "We're so eager to meet the family."

"Thanks," Phil said, with a glance toward the living room, lowering his voice. "I'm sure you know the Project cost my father-in-law his life. He killed himself this time last year. It brought Mutti to her knees." Phil looked over his glasses at Tom, then at Chiara. "We try not to talk about it much." He cleared his throat. "Anna and I think it's important not to upset Mutti and frighten her with other...ideas."

"We know, and we're so sorry for the family's loss," Chiara said as they trailed Phil down the hallway. Hmm. So, Phil goes for the suicide story. But maybe neither Zimmer nor Frau Wilhelm. An overly protective son-in-law? A head-in-the-sand kind of guy? Whatever he was, she and Tom mustn't provoke the fellow. Still, if Frau Wilhelm guessed the truth—and Zimmer may have already told her—. She left the thought hanging.

In the living room, Chiara looked around admiringly. Two rose-colored sofas, shiny with age, faced each other. To one side four deep armchairs encircled a Turkish coffee table. On the table, a dog-eared paperback thriller lay open and spine-up on top of an empty box of Swiss chocolates. A threadbare Persian carpet, its pattern too faded to read, stretched from wall to wall. In the low light of the late afternoon Chiara felt the room cast a vaguely unsettling spell.

Chiara guessed they'd entered a family shrine. The walls of the room dripped with memories. Faded photographs of men in military uniforms, women in high-necked, frilled dresses, and children in Buster Browns. Crumbling lithographs of temples and aqueducts. Dried edelweiss and cornflower preserved behind glass.

Chiara spotted the back of a woman with short salt and pepper hair bent over a baby grand. Swirling, soaring bars of music filled her ears. Phil said, "Mutti, our guests have arrived."

Frau Wilhelm's fingers lifted from the keyboard like feathers catching an updraft. A last sentimental note clung to life, then vanished. Her body seemed welded to her music as she swung her legs around the piano bench. A wide smile—flashing with gold inlays—brightened her face. Behind reading glasses blue and gray eyes flickered with intelligence. A long brown skirt, white cardigan over blue blouse, and scuffed brogues gave a sense of sober practicality.

Frau Wilhelm stood up and offered Chiara her hand. "Welcome my dears," she said, drawing Chiara into an embrace. She shook Tom's hand, waving him and Phil toward armchairs. "You men talk amongst yourselves," she said, bidding Chiara to take a sofa seat next to her. "Zimmer has told me everything, dear. I feel I know you already." She spoke a polished Oxford English. "Wait! Where's the little girl?"

"In the kitchen with Anna," Chiara said, stepping past the sofa to the piano, "You were playing Bach. It was lovely."

"Thank, you. *The English Suite Number One in A Major*. My husband's favorite. Do you know the work?"

"Yes," Chiara said. "As a young girl I studied at the San Diego Music Conservatory. Perhaps one day you'll invite me over to play."

"Of course. We'll arrange it," Frau Wilhelm said, linking arms with Chiara and nudging her toward a sofa seat. "Philip said you landed in Luxembourg a few days ago." She took a seat next to Chiara on the sofa.

"Yes," Chiara said. "Then we took the night train to Göttingen."

"A long journey, especially for the child," Frau Wilhelm sighed. "You must be tired." She threw back her shoulders and folded her hands on her lap. "I promised Professor Zimmer to welcome his Americans as if they were my own children. And I do so with all my heart." For a split-second Frau Wilhelm's eyes picked out Phil. Chiara thought she saw a gleam of defiance in Mutti's eyes. Had their hostess bucked her children with the promise to Zimmer to take in a family of strangers? Another landmine.

Chapter Four

Göttingen, December 1966

Tom turned away from Phil and looked at Frau Wilhelm, who had just broken into their conversation. "I'm sure you know this," she said to Tom. "Before the war my husband studied theology with Zimmer and Dabelstein. Served side by side with them on the Russian front. Survived a gulag." Her voice dropped. "That was long ago."

"We know the story from Zimmer," Chiara said.

"Mutti," Phil broke in, "That's all in the past. Best to leave it there." Damn. Now I've lost the quote I wanted to share with Tom."

"Sorry," Frau Wilhelm said, "I just wanted Tom to know my feelings. He, Chiara, and the child must think of themselves as part of our family." She turned to Chiara. "Please call me 'Mutti'."

"Thank you. I will."

Phil sputtered. "Gosh, that was quick. Welcome to the tribe."

Tom reached for Mutti's hand and gave it a warm squeeze. "We're so grateful to you and your family for taking us in. Finding an apartment is huge," Tom said.

"All is arranged." Frau Wilhelm beamed as she reached for a pack of HB cigarettes, handing the smokes to Tom and Chiara. Phil flicked a butane lighter and lit their cigarettes. "A local contractor named Herr Knobloch built the row of apartments behind my house," she said. "There is a vacancy, and he has promised it to you."

Tom said, "What wonderful news, right Chiara?" It was, she said.

Anna's head poked through the kitchen door. "Teatime," she announced. "Faith sits at the table already and samples everything. She's a darling."

Tom and Chiara walked behind Mutti and Phil into the dining room. After they'd settled in chairs around a gate leg table, Anna brought coffee and tea along with platters of gingersnaps, sugar cookies, and toasted cheese sandwiches. "Anna, this is Tom and Chiara," Mutti said. "Tom, Chiara, this is my daughter Anna."

"We met at the front door," Anna laughed. "Pleased to meet you."

"Likewise," Chiara said. What a lovely table you've set for tea. The Bruges lace tablecloth is exquisite. And look at that tasty cherry torte on the sideboard. Anna you are a wonderful cook."

"Thank you. I have a fine teacher." She gave Mutti's arm a pinch.

Mutti poured tea and coffee and told her family about their guest's journey to Göttingen.

Phil said, "Pity Anna and I leave for Oxford around New Year's Day. But it looks like Mutti won't miss us at all now that she's got three new family members to keep her company."

"Phil, behave yourself," Mutti chided her son-in-law. "Of course, I'll miss you two. But holidays are difficult when you're old and alone."

With tea over, Anna and Phil offered to do the cleanup. "Thank you, children," Mutti said, pushing away from the table. As she stood up, she motioned to Tom. "Let's go into my husband's study. Chiara, too. Anna, will you kindly keep an eye on Faith?"

Tom and Chiara followed Mutti into a small alcove off the living room. They pulled up at a delicate cherry wood writing desk and cane chair that faced an arched window with a gauzy curtain. Mutti stroked the back of the chair, lovingly. Tom heard a comforting, purring sound. He looked around for a cat. It was Mutti.

"So, this is where your husband worked," Tom said.

"Yes," Mutti said. "After he returned from Russia in 1952 I only saw his back for the last fourteen years of his life. But how could I blame him? He'd lost so many years of his academic life in the war and in the gulag." Mutti's hands dropped to the desktop. She caressed an emerald-green fountain pen. "You know, he told me almost nothing about his hunt for the lost letter. I hope you will help me understand why it led to his death. Anna and Phil consider the matter closed. I do not."

Tom let Mutti's remark hang in the air. His eyes met Chiara's as if they both heard something new and fraught with danger.

Ever so gently, Mutti picked up a pair of wire rimmed eyeglasses. She cleaned the lenses with a hanky she'd tucked into her belt then returned the glasses to the desktop. Sadness gathered like a line of clouds in her eyes, and Tom felt pulled in two directions at once. He and Chiara had swooped in while the family still grieved and puzzled over the death of a husband and father. At the same time, Mutti welcomed them warmly, found an apartment, and now showed them her husband's private papers.

Mutti held out the pen, couching it in both hands. "I think my husband would want you to have his favorite writing instrument."

"I can't take that," Tom demurred. "It means too much to you. And Anna and Phil."

"My husband would want it so. It will be as if he still writes about the Project with it. Besides, Anna hardly knew her father. She was already a teenager when he returned."

"Thank you," Tom said, slipping the pen into his shirt pocket. "I'm honored. I hope I can live up to your trust."

Chiara whispered in his ear. "Mutti just passed you a baton for the race we're running."

Mutti picked up a worn leather valise on the floor under the desk. She unlocked its clasp with a key that hung around her neck. "Inside are the journals and notebooks I told Zimmer about." She rifled through the contents. "Pocket diaries, leather-bound journals, sheafs of papers tied up with string," she said, handing Tom the key. "I'll go now. Zimmer asked me to find one of Anna's gowns for Chiara and a smoking jacket for you, Tom. For his upcoming lecture. There's also a winter coat that belonged to my husband."

"Please stay for a minute," Tom said. "It will save

time. I have a question."

"Of course."

"Did your husband ever mention a riddle in connection with the lost letter? "Two equals three, three equals two."

"Yes. He dismissed the riddle as nonsense. Say, what's this?" Mutti asked, picking up a letter that had fallen from the valise onto the floor. "It's postmarked Venice. On January 5 of last year. My husband died on January 15. I log all his mail. I've not seen it before."

"May I?" asked Tom, reaching for the letter, his curiosity overriding manners. He slipped a page out of the envelope. It bore the coat of arms of a monastery in Venice—Saint Lazarus of the Armenians. The writer was the monastery's librarian, Father Samvel. "Can you tell us what it says?" Tom asked. "It's in Italian."

Mutti reached for the letter. "The librarian sends fraternal greetings to my husband. He says it is a matter of some urgency to travel to the monastery. For the moment he's able to keep the *Panario*n safely in the library. But he cannot promise to do so much longer. He writes about vague threats." Mutti's hand flew to her mouth. "Why did my husband keep this letter from me? Why didn't he tell me about going to Venice?"

Chiara put her arms around Mutti. "He had your safety in mind, I'm sure."

"Mutti," Tom said, "this letter comes from the same person in the monastery who loaned Professor Gordon and me the *Panarion* a few months ago."

"Father Samvel," Chiara said.

Tom said, "We think that Samvel wanted us to

safeguard the book from thieves. But the university couldn't afford the insurance premium so back it went to Venice."

"Father Samvel wrote my husband, pleading with him to come to Venice? To save the book?" Mutti's face knotted with confusion.

"Yes, Mutti," Tom said, "that's my strong hunch. Are you're sure you didn't know about a trip to Venice? Or, why?"

"No," she said. "I didn't know. I made all his travel arrangements. He never mentioned Venice. We had no secrets." Her lips trembled as she gathered up the Project records and returned them to the valise. "Was he killed because of this letter?"

Tom shook his head. "I don't know." Truth was Wilhelm's show of interest in the *Panarion* and the letter on its last three pages may have led to his death. But a grieving widow didn't deserve more sorrow. Wilhelm may have kept his planned trip to Venice a secret because there was danger involved. And for some reason he hadn't confided in Zimmer or Dabelstein either.

Tom said. "May I keep the letter and show Professor Zimmer?"

"Of course."

A shadow crossed the alcove as Anna walked in. "I'm sorry to bother you, Tom. Mutti must lie down. Talking about father's work is very painful." She reached for the pen sticking out of Tom's pocket. "I see you've inherited my father's pen and valise, too. I'm glad. He was a fine scholar. You will turn out to be one, too."

"Of course, he will," Chiara said, slipping a hand around Tom's arm.

"Faith waits with Phil at the front door," Anna said. "I have tied the evening clothes up in a bundle for you. Also, father's winter coat." She looped a hand around her mother's arm. "You two give us hope. Perhaps one day you will answer our many questions about Father's work and death. God speed you both."

Mutti, swaying slightly, stepped over to her daughter. As they left the room, she looked back at Tom and Chiara. Her mouth formed a word: Venice. She touched a finger to her lips. Tom dipped his head to show he understood. Next stop: Venice. Before the *Panarion* and its precious Papyrus went missing for good.

Chapter Five

Göttingen, January 1967

A week before Zimmer's lecture to the Göttingen Academy, Valdo Kammer threw a handful of dirt onto his mother's coffin. Woodenly, he watched as the grave hole swallowed the pine box. Then, without waiting for the burial to end, he slipped away from the churchyard and peddled back on his bicycle to his farm.

He was glad to be rid of the old woman who'd lain in bed these three years past, more vegetable than human since her stroke. Now, he could sell the farm with its thirty hardscrabble hectares, rotting barn, smoky and low-slung house. For years, he'd dreamed of a modern flat in nearby Göttingen. Central heating. Warm water. Linen sheets. Gas stove. Supermarkets. With cash in his strongbox, he'd learn to travel. Perhaps even as far as Vienna or Prague for strudel and schnitzel and a decent bottle of cherry brandy.

When Valdo reached the farm, he stowed his bike in the old barn and saw to the slop for the pigs and the grain for the chickens. He was a brick of a fellow, a hardworking, muscular man who deadlifted hundred-kilogram sheep into a farm cart. Neighbors knew him for a crack shot with his Mauser hunting rifle.

Years before, he and five other thirteen-year-olds from the parish joined the Hitler Youth Movement. They'd spent the summer of 1935 working on the construction of a fine amphitheater in the hills above Heidelberg. Shoveling and carting dirt. Laying lines for the benches and flag stones. Sawing and carting timber for the stage. Oh, what a glorious summer that had been! Helping to build an outdoor stadium for Herr Hitler's rallies. Perhaps one day he'd revisit the place. He'd heard that nowadays students and tourists trashed the stadium, camping and drinking and fornicating, even mounting rock concerts. The papers mocked the structure and called it the Thing-Site.

Well, no need to dwell on the past. A bright future lay ahead. In fact, in the past two years he'd already proven his worth to the Sodality. Twice. On one of those occasions, he'd thrown a Göttingen theology professor named Wilhelm out a university library window. It tickled his fancy to relive the moment. The old man falling, arms and legs clawing the air, screams fading to silence as the walkway rose up to meet the body. True, the blood splatter did not live up to his expectations. Still how much juice did a dried-up old professor have left?

On the same Sunday that Valdo buried his mother, Professor Zimmer attended a church service and luncheon with his wife. He excused himself shortly after noon to leave for campus. There were lecture notes for the Academy presentation to polish up. And he had a meeting with Tom Weathering.

Locked in his office he worked until late afternoon on his notes. By the time the library's carillon chimed 4 p.m. shadows crawled the walls. He reached to turn on his desk lamp and heard a rustling in the open doorway. Looking up from his desk, he caught his breath, and a hand flew to his mouth. In the door to his office stood a ghost: Martin Wilhelm in his familiar winter coat, his leather briefcase dangling from his left hand. "No!" Zimmer said under his breath, swiping an eye with the back of his hand.

"Trouble, sir?" Tom asked.

Zimmer blinked and blew out his cheeks. "Tom. My God. You just gave me a scare. Where'd you get that coat and valise?"

"Oh these," Tom said. "Mutti. Gave them to me along with a fountain pen." He tapped a cylinder shape in his breast pocket. "She said my anorak was too thin. Overcoat belonged to her husband. You OK?"

"Well, I am now," Zimmer said, reaching for a Pervitin tablet. "For an instant, I saw Wilhelm in the doorway. You're about his height and build."

"Wow, that's a trip," Tom said. "Sure you're OK?"

"Thank you. I am now." Zimmer pointed Tom to the sofa. "You'll have to remove that box of archeological debris from the cushions. Lisle's away until next week. Otherwise, I'd offer coffee."

"No problem. I had a cup an hour ago with Chiara."

"How was your first German Christmas with Frau Wilhelm and family?" Zimmer asked.

"Magical. Christmas Eve we helped Phil and Anna

decorate Mutti's tree. Faith lit the candles on the low-hanging branches. Still talks about it. At midnight we attended the Bach Oratorio at church. Christmas Day, Mutti served roast goose in a cranberry sauce. I think I drank too much cherry brandy."

Zimmer chuckled. "Easy to do," he said, "I spoke with her two days ago. She has virtually adopted you three, hasn't she?"

"Feels like it. Phil says there's a happiness in her eyes that's been gone since her husband passed. And a bit of good news: we have an apartment directly behind her home."

Zimmer's face flushed with pleasure. He hadn't missed the reference to "Mutti." She'd gathered the Americans under her wing, more or less sight-unseen, and settled them in like a mother hen. Good signs, all. "Excellent," Zimmer said. "Frau Wilhelm moves mountains. Anything else?"

"Mutti says we can move into the apartment in a couple of weeks. And she showed me some of her husband's journals and diaries."

"I've seen most of them."

"Mm, maybe not this." Tom unclasped the valise, pulled out the letter that had fallen on the floor in Wilhelm's study. He handed it to Zimmer. "It's from someone you might remember from your visit ten years ago to the Venice monastery. Name's Father Samvel."

"Yes, I recall the man. Monastery librarian. At the time he refused to loan us the *Panarion*. But he did photograph the last three folios that contained the

Armenian text of the Letter to the Laodiceans."

Tom said, "Samvel is a close relative of Sona Routanian, our missing translator. She persuaded Samvel to loan Marquette the *Panarion* last October." Tom pointed to the postmark on the envelope. "Check this out. Professor Wilhelm received this letter just before he died last year. It begged him to come to Venice and collect the *Panarion.*"

Zimmer read the letter twice before handing it back to Tom. Wisps of a conversation skittered across his mind. Just before Wilhelm died, he'd hinted at an urgent trip to Venice. His reason? A niggling suspicion that someone might steal or destroy the *Panarion*. As far as he, Zimmer, knew Wilhelm never went to Venice.

Zimmer said, "The letter surprises me. Of course, I knew that Wilhelm planned to meet Father Samvel. I warned him not to go alone and to take a younger colleague for safety's sake."

"Safety's sake?"

"Look, the *Panarion* will lead us to the actual letter, what you call the Androgyne Papyrus. Whoever finds the writing will release lightening from a bottle. Its message will mobilize women of faith everywhere. Children abused by clergy will hire attorneys. And each of those efforts brings great danger, Tom. Do you understand that you and Chiara must have a care?" Zimmer said nothing for a long moment. He stared at his hands in a kind of electric silence.

"Professor Zimmer...?" Tom asked. "You OK?"

"Sorry. Just thinking about Wilhelm. I miss the man so much. You have a question?"

"Not a question. A decision. I'm taking Chiara and

Faith to Venice. You and I owe that much to Mutti, Gordon, and Wilhelm. And the Project. We're off as soon as we settle into the apartment."

Zimmer blinked in surprise. "Like hell you are. Too dangerous."

"Sir, you know as well as I do; we need to get our hands on the *Panarion*. That silly riddle about three equals two and two equals three actually may mean something."

Zimmer wagged his head. "Gordon said you could be zealous, Tom. He didn't tell me you were foolhardy as well."

"Look, we need to find a way to surgically open those last three folios in the *Panarion*. If they are really envelope pages, we may find the lost letter." Tom grinned and said, "So what do you say?"

Zimmer rubbed a knuckle across his mouth. Thank God for Pervitin. He could at least think straight and keep up with the young American's boundless energy. "You give me fits today," he said. "The thought of your going to Venice alone…" Zimmer broke off and looked away. There had been a day when he'd have bolted without hesitation for Venice. Now, crippled and old, he could only look on.

"Sir?"

"…makes me feel like a deserter." He took a pen from his vest pocket and rubbed it between his hands as if he were rolling out thoughts in his mind. What a bitter irony that Wilhelm survived the war and gulag only to meet his death when he decided to look for a biblical book in a holy monastery. Yet that monastery held the key to finding the letter. Zimmer put the pen down and ran a finger along the scar on his face. "Know how we used to settle these matters when I was a student and member of a fencing club?"

"No sir, not really."

"With three feet of Damascus steel. Nothing like a glittering blade pressed to your chest to clarify the mind." He grinned wolfishly at Tom.

"Wouldn't know about that, sir. Back home we just flip a coin."

Zimmer laughed, long and hard. "That felt good."

"So, you do agree?" Tom said. "You'll send us?"

"You've boxed me in. Wilhelm's dead. Dabelstein and I too busy or feeble to travel. That leaves me with you and Chiara. 'Do I agree?' you ask. No, dammit, I don't agree. Do I have a better suggestion? No. That's the rub." Zimmer heaved an exasperated sigh. "When Lisle returns after the break, she'll arrange things with the authorities here at the university and in Italy." He opened a drawer in a side table and reached for a Schnapps bottle and two glasses.

"So, all set for the Academy lecture?" Tom said, holding out his hand for a glass.

Valdo Kammer leaned over a dessert table in the parish hall of Saint Peter's church. With a ladle he scooped whipped cream from a ceramic bowl onto his plate of ginger cake. As he forked up a first bite, he saw his Sodality contact, a man named Anton Griessmer, stride into the hall, brush snow off his coat, and point toward a door that led to the kitchen.

A woman standing at a deep sink full of suds and dirty dishes gave the two men a broad smile. Griessmer sent the woman away. Throwing the dead bolt on the door, he pulled up two chairs next to a crackling pot-bellied stove. "Sit," he ordered. For a few minutes the two men talked about the weather and the local football club. Then Griessmer handed Valdo a fat envelope.

Valdo slit the envelope with a pen knife and ran his thumb across the crisp edges of ten new fifty Mark bills. Behind the last bill lay a folded sheet of paper with a typewritten note: PROFESSOR WALTHER ZIMMER. OLD HALL. UNIVERSITY. JANUARY 15. 8 P.M.

"Memorize the note then burn it," Griessmer said, opening the stove door and tossing in a shuttle of coal. Embers flashed at the mouth. He slammed the door shut with a bang. "Now listen carefully. You must time the shot exactly. The lecture begins at 8 p.m. sharp. And the kill must happen no later than 8:45 p.m. Before guests start to leave. We want maximum uproar. Exit the Old Hall well before the lecture begins. Two days from now a courier will deliver a rifle, tripod, and scope to the farm.

Valdo, put off by the lordly tone of the Sodality man, studied his calloused hands. "My fee," he said, "has doubled since I took care of the professor in the Göttingen library. And what's this about leaving the projection room before the shot. Are you crazy?"

"How dare you speak to me like that? Mind your manners, Valdo. You're just a workman for the Sodality. First things first," Griessmer said, standing up and pulling a roll of bills from his jacket pocket. "Here. This money is a deposit. Do the job well, and I'll add more."

Valdo stood up, too, and took a step toward Griessmer.

He stood inches taller than the man and outweighed him by twenty pounds at least. How easy it would be to pick him up like one of his hogs and snap his back. Instead, he jabbed a finger against a button on the man's wool jacket. "How in the hell do I pull off a kill if I'm not in the room? You must be crazy."

Griessmer stepped back and squeezed a Sodality pin on his lapel between a thumb and forefinger. A cross overlaid with a skull adorned the pin. "Remember, Valdo, I stand here in place of the abbot."

Valdo snorted. Best not to push the man. He needed the work. "OK. Forget it. But you talk in riddles."

Griessmer said, "Your equipment kit includes an automatic timing and firing device. Set the timer for 8:45 p.m. It's child's play. You'll have no problem."

"And how do I gain entry to the Old Hall?"

"Show up at the service entrance the morning of the lecture. You're a repair man scheduled to replace a window frame in the projection booth at the back of the Old Hall."

"I don't like this one bit," Valdo said. "I always make the kill myself."

"Another time, Valdo. The Sodality has many such assignments. You can be of much use to us."

Chapter Six

On Wednesday morning of the lecture, Valdo knocked on the half-open service door to the Old Hall. The door swung open. A cloud of schnapps spiraled around the custodian inside. A miniature poodle, bows tied to each ear, snuggled in the man's arms. The custodian waved Valdo in, jabbing a finger toward a winding staircase down the hall. "That'll take you to the projection room at the back of the Old Hall." He belched and said, "The window up there has needed a good repair for ages. There's a cart in the corner if you want to load it with your tools."

"Thank you. Make sure no one disturbs me," Valdo said.

"Of course."

By early afternoon, Valdo had replaced a rusted frame. A crank handle, newly oiled, spun easily and worked the window with smoothness. Valdo looked out into the Old Hall. There was a clear view of the stage one hundred feet away. From a hidden compartment in the base of his tool chest, Valdo lifted out the barrel and stock of a .22 caliber rifle and a high-powered Weatherby scope. The rifle's barrel and bolt action smelled of minty gun oil.

Valdo loved the sharp scent that stung his nostrils and focused his mind on a kill. He spread out a clean flannel cloth and placed on it a modified Lafette tripod and a single hollow-head bullet. For the past week, he'd practiced marksmanship with one of his own .22 rifles. Two dozen squirrels and rabbits and even a red fox hung by their tails in his tractor shed.

He assembled the rifle and extended the legs of the tripod to the height of the windowsill, shimmying one leg to level it on the floor. The threaded opening in the rifle stock rotated smoothly onto the machine screw on the tripod head. He locked the scope on the rifle barrel and twisted a homemade silencer onto the muzzle. Turning the scope's twin dials, Valdo corrected for elevation. Then he squared up the crosshairs exactly where he placed Zimmer's head above the lectern.

The timer and firing device lay in a corner, still packaged. It wronged Valdo's sense of the killing craft to leave the work to a timer and firing device. He'd decided to make the kill himself. When it was all over, he'd put on a borrowed dinner jacket and join the rest of the guests running for their lives out of the Old Hall. Already he pictured the horror on their faces.

Valdo settled down comfortably in a battered rocking chair to wait. He reached for a bottle of beer and a ham sandwich on the cart. See you soon Professor Zimmer.

That evening, Zimmer hailed a taxi to drive him to the Old

Hall. When he arrived, a porter in bright-buttoned livery met the car and brought a wheelchair. Zimmer waved the man off. "I'll stand at the lectern tonight, Johann. Keep the chair close."

"Yes, sir, Professor," the porter said with a snappy military salute. He followed Zimmer toward the stage entrance of the Old Hall, leaving him in the wings awaiting an introduction.

At 8:00 p.m. sharp, the Academy president arrived on stage to introduce Zimmer. A thin, florid-faced man, he took mincing steps toward the dais. Above and behind him hung gallery-sized portraits on the wall. He paused and dipped his head to the figure of King George II, the university's founder. Climbing onto the dais, he swept his eyes over the packed hall. "This evening," he began, "our honored lecturer is Walther Zimmer, professor of Biblical Archaeology and Old Testament." After reading out Zimmer's record of honors and publications, he said, "Please help me welcome our honored speaker."

"We're on Old Henry," Zimmer said as he climbed onto the stage. At the lectern, he adjusted a gooseneck lamp and looked out into the Old Hall. As often as he'd spoken in this exquisite room, he still felt awed. Twenty French Empire chandeliers hung from the ceiling like a galaxy of noonday suns. The floor, a checkerboard of red and orange Tuscan marble, returned the light and splashed it against the chairs.

He scanned the box seats between the ochre and white colonnades that ran the length of the side aisles. No Tom and Chiara. Then he found them second row center on the

43

auditorium floor. Chiara sparkled in her sequined gown and Tom looked dashing in a smoking jacket. A handsome couple. Frau Wilhelm did the Americans proud.

Pulling out his pocket watch, Zimmer wound its stem and placed it face up next to his notes. "Thank you, Professor Neuman, for the kind introduction." Zimmer spoke in a commanding voice, deep and full chested. "Over a year ago we lost our friend and colleague Martin Wilhelm. I dedicate this lecture to his memory and life's work. I'd also like to honor Martin's life and work by breaking with tradition and not giving the usual formal lecture followed by a Q&A. This evening, I want to invite you to ask questions as we go along."

Behind Zimmer gears ground as a screen dropped down. From a projector in the orchestra pit a beam of light flashed and filled the screen. WILL THE REAL JESUS CHRIST PLEASE STAND UP? read the title bar on the first slide. "Next slide please," Zimmer said.

A grainy, black and white photo popped up. "That's Father Damian," Zimmer said. "On his gulag deathbed he revealed a great secret. It was the location of the *Panarion,* an ancient book of heresies. Its last three leaves preserve in Armenian a lost letter of Apostle Paul."

"That's the writing that set off violent attacks among Jews, Christians, and Muslims," a man in the first row shouted.

"One and the same," Zimmer replied, evenly. "We can talk about that if you wish."

"Why did the letter trigger so much violence?" the man asked.

"Fair enough," Zimmer said. "Because it presents Jesus as an androgyne, a male-female figure. And just as explosive, it calls for women to help lead the early church."

"Thank you," the guest said.

"He-she figures are not foreign to the Bible," Zimmer began, gesturing for the next slide to come up. With his laser pointer he underlined several biblical passages. "Some rabbis of the biblical period read these texts as references to androgenous figures." He tapped on Genesis 3:12 where Eve was a *he* and on Genesis 9:21 where Noah was a *she*.

"I know another interesting case," said a young woman on the right side of the auditorium. "Rebecca becomes a 'young man' in Genesis 24:6."

"Thank you," Zimmer said. "I missed that one completely."

A man next to the young woman leaped to his feet. "But what if those rabbis are wrong? Or the translation is off?"

"Point taken," Zimmer said, calmly. "But forget about the Hebrew Bible for a moment. We know that Apostle Paul spoke and wrote Greek and had a passing knowledge of classical art and literature of the day. It's even odds he knew about statues of androgynes or as the Romans called such figures 'hermaphrodites'." A CLICK brought up the Borghese Hermaphrodite housed at the Louvre. The slide percolated for a moment on the screen before Zimmer went on. "In this slide a nude female figure, her male genitalia in plain sight, stretches out on a plush buttoned mattress."

"And the whole work commissioned by no less a figure than Cardinal Scipione Borghese," an audience member hooted from a gallery box.

Zimmer grinned as a ripple of laughter passed through the Hall. He felt the pressure of the evening ease off. "No shortage of hermaphrodites for Paul to study," he said, "if the apostle wanted to write about one in his letters."

"Now, let's put Saint Paul and the androgyne Jesus aside for the moment. I want to talk about the upshot of a male Jesus in modern history and culture. How many of you enjoyed *The Greatest Story Ever Told* when it screened in town last year?" Dozens of hands shot up. "Did you question the casting of Max von Sydow, the blond, blue-eyed Swedish actor who played the role of Jesus, a short, dark-skinned Palestinian Jew?" The guests shook their heads save a few who nodded.

"Of course, most of you didn't," Zimmer said. "And now a more pointed, even painful question. Can you imagine that an Anglo-Saxon male Jesus might help give rise to racism, genocide, sexism, pedophilia, and other crimes against humanity?"

A dead silence wrapped the auditorium. A few guests cleared their throats. Others looked at their fingernails or wristwatches.

Zimmer let the thought sit with his audience for a moment. Then he said, "Surely, we Germans remember that a mixture of Nazi politics and Aryan theology led to the destruction of European Jews."

The silence thickened in the auditorium. No one moved. Zimmer wondered if he was the only person breathing. Then some of the guests let out whistling breaths. A row of guests stood up and walked out. Zimmer cleared his throat and took a slow sip of water while his eyes roamed the Old Hall. "Now, I'm going to take you around the world to other cultures that have represented Jesus in ways very different from our own."

For the next thirty minutes Zimmer discussed the images he'd previewed with Tom and Chiara. A beardless, teen-age Jesus wearing a tunic, dressed as a shepherd. A nude boy in a rippling pool of clear water. A bearded, adult image of Christ the All-Powerful. A thin Negroid figure of the Ethiopian Coptic Church. The Jamaican Rastafarian Jesus. Quetzalcoatl, the Mayan feathered serpent Jesus. The crucified Christ of the Kongo people.

As the Kongo image faded away, a man in the back row screamed, "This is grotesque. This is madness." He scuffled with his seat mates, clambered over chairs, ran down the center aisle. He vaulted on the stage and charged the dais, waving a long, murderous-looking blade back and forth. "If God won't punish you, I will," he screamed as he reached the dais and plunged the blade into the lectern.

By the time the crazed man had reached the stage, Tom had already jumped over several rows of seats and vaulted onto the stage. He barreled toward the protestor, threw him to the stage floor and twisted the knife from his hand, gashing his own palm. "Easy now, fellah," he said to the man as he put an arm lock around his neck. "I've got him, sir. At least for a moment. You OK?"

Zimmer nodded. "Thanks, Tom. I think so. Guess I wasn't ready for a knife fight. You're bleeding."

"I'm good," Tom said as he staunched the blood on his hand with a silk handkerchief Mutti had tucked into his vest pocket.

"Oh no, you're not," Chiara said joining Tom on the dais. "You're going to need some stitches. You're not Fearless Fosdick."

Two security guards led the attacker off the stage then walked Tom and Chiara to a first-aid room. On the stage Zimmer composed himself. He looked at his watch: 8:45 p.m. His good knee throbbed, and Old Henry felt like a pillar of lead pulling on his hip. Still, he'd stay for a few questions. He owed the audience that much. He waved to the porter who rushed to the lectern with the wheelchair and eased Zimmer onto its cushioned seat.

High above the stage in the projection room, Valdo checked his watch: 8:43 p.m. "Take it slow, take it slow," he said under his breath as he chambered the cartridge. "Plenty of time for a clean shot." He squinted through the scope, lining up crosshairs on the center of Zimmer's head. His finger, feather-light on the trigger, curled as he took a deep breath to steady himself to get off the shot.

Damn. Valdo blinked with surprise. A man wielding a knife had rushed the stage and a second man wrestled him to the ground. From the wings a porter pushed a wheelchair toward the lectern. He paused to load Zimmer in the conveyance. There was no clear line of sight.

Valdo chanced his shot. The porter fell over on top of Zimmer, knocking him and his wheelchair to the floor.

Valdo squeezed into an ill-fitting dinner jacket and melted into the crowd rushing for the exit doors.

Chapter Seven

Göttingen. January 1967

It was a Monday morning—six days after the Old Hall shooting—before Tom saw Zimmer again. And that was only at the invitation of Inspector Carolyn Arendt of Göttingen's Major Incident Team, who'd called a briefing in Zimmer's office.

Stepping into the room, Tom's jaw dropped. The place was a mash-up and smelled of mildew and dust and alcohol. He covered a sneeze with a shirtsleeve. Where orderly bookcases and credenzas once reigned, a frenzied disorder now ruled. Books teetered on shelves. Cabinet doors swung on their hinges. Files lay strewn across the floor. He whispered to Lisle, Zimmer's assistant, "What the hell happened?"

Lisle took Tom's coat and slung it on a rack. "Burglars? Vandals? Students? No one knows." She dabbed at tears in her eyes, offering Tom a seat on the sofa next to Zimmer's box of shards. "Happened the day after the lecture."

Settling on a seat next to Tom, Lisle gave a thin smile, blew her nose, and tucked a hanky into her sweater sleeve.

Words tumbled out in broken English. "Everything kaput ...Professor Zimmer is like...like a crazy man. I try to help ...to clean up...he shouts at me: 'I can take care of it. I need my army pistol. Get out.' I think he's frightened and trying to look brave." She paused before adding, "He refuses police protection. I'm so scared. I have a child at home." She swallowed a sob and buried her face in her hands.

Tom put an arm around the terrified woman's shoulder. "You're safe now. The cops are here," he said. He took in the scene, his mouth flattening into hard, worried lines. Zimmer, bent over his desk, flicked his ridge of bushy eyebrows up and down like a storefront awning in the wind. He tapped a pencil idly on a blotter as if the only threat to his life was boredom. The inspector, dressed in a gabardine pants suit and work boots, looked seasoned and tough. She paced back and forth in front of Zimmer's desk. A second detective hovered near her, shooting photos of the crime scene with a 35mm Leica.

"So, professor," the inspector said, "Weathering has finally arrived. Now we begin. First, I review our initial findings," she said, flipping open her battered notepad. "In the Old Hall the crime scene investigators found a .22 caliber casing, rifle, tripod, and scope in the rear projection room. Timing device, too. Not used. Yesterday, forensics reported no readable serial numbers. No fingerprints or any other physical evidence of the shooter, either. A cleaned-up crime scene. Likely a professional hit." She paused and asked Zimmer if he was paying attention. To Tom, the smile that Zimmer returned looked more like a smirk. Tom listened dutifully to a dreary account of house-to-house searches near Old Hall. In spite of himself he shuddered when the inspector asked Zimmer to go over one last time the details of the assault in the Old Hall.

"Thank you, Professor Zimmer," the inspector said when Zimmer finished. "Bottom line," she added, looking right at Zimmer, "you need police protection. You've not seen the last of these people."

"Inspector Arendt," Zimmer said in a voice warped by too much early morning Schnapps, "Forget it. Save the taxpayer money." He tapped the pistol grip of a Luger. "I can take care of myself." A box of 9mm cartridges and a clip lay next to the weapon. "Just filled the clip."

The policewoman reached for the pistol then pulled back. "You have a permit?" She didn't wait for an answer and went on. "The American on the sofa? His family? What about their safety?"

"The Americans? Ach, they're safe enough," Zimmer said, wearily." They're leaving town for a few days."

Safe enough? Tom didn't believe his ears. He was glad Chiara had stayed back in the hotel. Zimmer was drunk and cut too shabby a figure for her to see. He leaned into Lisle. "Didn't the custodian give a description of the shooter? Come on, pull yourself together."

"Him? A freakin', bloody drunk," Lisle spat out. "Worthless piece of shit. Totally blanked out."

The policewoman reached for her overcoat on the back of a nearby chair and said to Zimmer, "Don't you understand, sir, smart man like you? The shooter escaped our dragnet and will strike again." She tossed a harried look over her shoulder at Tom. "I asked you here to help with Zimmer. Do what you can with the man. He's got a death wish."

"Waste of time," Zimmer shot back. "I can look after myself. Survived the Russians, didn't I? Besides, your assassin can't shoot straight. Missed me, musta nicked the portrait of King George behind me on the stage."

"Sir," Tom said, now troubled about Zimmer's head space, "the porter took the shot meant for you. Thank God, he's recovering in the hospital." Tom heaved himself up from the couch. His anger at Zimmer hung in the air, as thick as the old man's cloud of alcohol. "Sir, listen to the police! The Sodality's behind this. You know what happened to Wilhelm. It was just dumb luck you sat down in your wheelchair when the shooter pulled the trigger."

"Piffle," Zimmer said, waving a scornful hand.

"Goodbye," the policewoman said to Zimmer as she turned to leave the office. "You know all we do. There is nothing more to say." She stepped to the sofa and blew out her cheeks. "Mr. Weathering, I know what's going on in the old man's head. The police have their hands full with these old veterans and their shell shock, alcoholism, guilt, domestic abuse. You name it. In his case, it's a Jesus complex. I don't like it, but I can't do anything about it."

"Huh? Jesus complex?" Tom said, gapping at the inspector, his nose a wrinkled slope. "What the hell is that?"

"Mind set of some old soldiers who're still stuck on the front lines. Did everything in the war to keep their comrades alive. Come home plagued with guilt over the ones they lost. Look for ways today to balance the scales."

"Do you think I could change his mind about the offer of protection?" Tom asked Lisle, who shrugged her shoulders. "He might listen to me."

"Ha, as if!" the inspector snorted. "Doubt it. Zimmer thinks you and your partner are in mortal danger—his words not ours—because of this Sodality thing. Way I figure it, he's got it in his skull that he's fending off the Sodality from you and your family. Wants the goons to target him and take their eyes off you folks."

God, poor old Zimmer, Tom thought. Caught up in fantasies that make his life bearable, he plays cat and mouse with killers. Come to think of it, that's what Gordon did when he arranged for them to leave Milwaukee.

Tom walked over to Zimmer and put his arm around his shoulder. "I can stay a while longer if you want to talk."

Lisle grabbed Tom's sleeve and pulled him away. "I'll stay with him. Not the first time I've had to nurse him a bit." She handed Tom his overcoat. "Come with me," she said. "I almost forgot. There's a letter for you on my desk. It came yesterday." She handed Tom a business-size envelope with a generic APO address.

"Thanks," Tom said, recognizing the block letters on the envelope. "It's from an old school friend. Mike Mathis." He stepped into the hallway and read the letter. He smothered a laugh at Mike's machine-gun style. "Good-bye Mekong River. No more IV Corps. VC mine sunk PBR. Scored a land berth. Patton Barracks. Near Heidelberg. Sweet. How's detecting? Need some muscle?"

Tom, glad for the letter, scratched his head: how the

hell had the guy slipped it by the Army's censors. All the banter about his movements might cost him a reprimand or worse. Well, even the army hadn't trimmed all his friend's wild hairs.

A clipping fell out of the envelope onto the floor, and Tom bent over to pick it up. Mike had scribbled REMEMBER HIM? over the headshot of his parish priest back in elementary school. Father Michael Cody. Tom read the article, and its news scorched his mouth, calling up a memory, vile and cancerous, that prickled across his scalp. Six boys, including Tom and Mike, and a lake cabin. Foot long hotdogs and tangy Kool-Aide. Campfire songs. Bunk room with too few bunks. The big bed in Father's room. The Yakima diocese had caught Cody red-handed abusing boys in the youth group. His punishment? Reassigned to a new parish. Chaplain to its Catholic Youth Organization and Cub Scout Pack. Tom wagged his head. It never changes. He crumpled the clipping and threw it into a trash can.

Anger blotched Tom's cheeks. He thought of Chiara. A victim herself, she somehow always knew the right thing to say. No time now, Tom, to put balm on our own wounds. We have bigger fish to fry. Venice. And she'd be right.

Tom pulled on his coat and wound his way through the old city to the Botanical Garden. He settled on a bench for ten minutes in the orchid greenhouse, putting his head in order. On a whim he plucked a filmy blossom, wrapped it in his handkerchief and left for the Gebhards Hotel.

He found Chiara and Faith kneeling on the floor, bottoms up, and looking for something under the bed.

Faith's puzzles covered a small area rug. He laughed. "You two make quite an impression on the casual visitor."

"We're looking for a missing piece under the bed. Help us. Please?"

"Sure, then let's walk into the old city for some lunch. I saw a shop with the remains of the Christmas holiday market. We'll pick up some gingerbread and sugar cookies for the train trip to Venice."

Chiara stood up and poked Tom's belly. "As if you needed more sweets."

"We should talk about this morning. The police are empty-handed, Zimmer waved a pistol around, and there's a letter from Mike."

"Will you help Faith and me pick out wallpaper for the new apartment before we leave for Venice?"

"Sure," Tom said, unfolding his handkerchief and handing Chiara the delicate blossom. "Fresh start."

Chapter Eight

Göttingen, January 1967

While Tom and Zimmer worked out the details of the trip to the Venice monastery, Chiara, Mutti, and Faith moved clothes and personal items out of the Gebhards Hotel and into their apartment. Barely settled in their new home, they packed and boarded an express for Venice. To their delight, Zimmer had upgraded their tickets to a private first-class compartment. Chiara's eyes lit up at a wicker basket of fruit and sandwiches on the fold-down table. GOOD LUCK AND GOD SPEED. Z. read a card pinned to its side.

Five hours later, the train braked for the Salzburg, Austria station, pulling onto a sidetrack for a show of passports and change of crew. "My stomach's growling," Tom said. "How 'bout you and Faith? You guys hungry?"

"Famished," Chiara said. "We've had nothing but Zimmer's fruit and sandwiches all day."

"Me hungry, too," Faith said with a belly rub. "Wanna hot dog."

"You, my little mouse, will eat with the other children. There's a fast snack area for kids and a nice nanny to play with. Mama and Papa have a lot to talk about over dinner."

Faith put a hand on her hip. "Wanna eat with Mama and Papa, God-dammit."

"Faith," Chiara shrieked. "Where'd you hear that kind of talk?"

"Papa. Hammer hit finger."

"Thomas Weathering!"

"I told her to say 'Gosh darn it' not 'God-dammit'." He shot Faith a guilty look that said they were both in trouble.

"No, Papa. Bad word Gosh-darn-it."

Tom rolled his eyes. "If I had any Fels Naptha soap," Chiara said, "I'd scrub both of your mouths. Can't have our kid cussing like a lumberjack in kindergarten."

They left Faith with a young nanny in the fast snack area and followed a maître'd to a linen-draped table in the dining car. "We left the apartment in quite a mess," Tom said as he helped Chiara with her chair and picked up a menu. "Thanks for doing the heavy lifting."

"It's fine. I love the apartment. There's going to be so much light in the three rooms, even in winter with all those tall windows."

"We've never had so much furniture," Tom said. "We owe Mutti and her neighbors a huge thank you."

"And how about those goose down comforters? Is there anything more snuggly than burying the three of us in their warmth?"

"Those lava lamps you turned up in the dumpster? Real classics."

Tom put on a show of reading the Italian menu while Chiara fingered a Dresden china dinner plate then turned over a crystal wine glass. "Look," she whispered, "Waterford. Reminds me of my parents' place setting. Maybe we should take up train travel and detecting full time."

Thirty minutes later, near the Italian border, there was a shift change in the dining car, and a schoolyard-like commotion filled the galley. Chiara glanced up at the throng of Italian cooks, dishwashers, and waiters replacing the German staff. With shoulder shrugs, wrist flips, and head slaps the new crew jostled into the dining car. A waiter with a pencil-thin mustache and a wide crescent of a smile approached their table.

"I am Giovanni," he said with a quick bow. "I will take care of you." As he fine-tuned the place settings to his liking, he explained that there was a German way and an Italian way to dress a table. "For you, it is the Italian way." An Austrian couple two tables away called Giovanni and he excused himself with an: "I am come back pronto."

For the first time in days, Tom felt his face muscles soften. Venice lay only a few hours south. He could smell the hay in the barn. Chiara tugged at the dinner menu. "I'll do the ordering."

"You sure?"

"I'm sure. Remember, I studied in Venice four...no five years ago."

"That's where you got that ankle tattoo I saw for the first time in the Mount Spokane ski lodge. That was many moons ago. Eager to see Venice again?"

Giovanni returned with a wine list. He looked at Tom who shook his head. Chiara said, "the Valpolicella."

The waiter sucked loudly on the bunched fingertips of one hand, producing an explosive kiss. "As you wish," he said and glided off.

When the wine arrived, Tom leaned over the table. "So, Venice. Rekindle some memories?"

"A few."

"Tell me more."

"There were ten of us," Chiara said, "mostly from the University of San Diego. It was the summer of 1962, between my freshman and sophomore years. We stayed in a hostel on the land side of the Palazzo Dario. That's where I met David. He was older and exotic and a sabra.

"Sabra?"

"A Jew born in Israel. Ex-paratrooper studying civil engineering. By the end of the second week, we'd become friends and hung out every day in the Rialto. He knew so much about the architecture and engineering of Venice. I'd never met anyone like him. Did you know—?"

Giovanni coughed and leaned over the table to check the level of the Valpolicella. He promised a second bottle with the main course. A savory smell clung to the waiter's livery, and Chiara inhaled deeply. It was, the waiter explained, a preparation for the evening's starter, scampi in a buttery cinnamon sauce. "I recommend it. After that a pasta marinara for the first plate, and an osso bucco for the second." Giovanni lifted his shoulders as if he wanted to levitate and said, "Our osso bucco falls apart on the bone and floats in saucy onions and carrots on a bed of zesty farina." Tom felt his mouth water.

After Giovanni left to place the order, Tom topped off

their wine glasses. "Did I know…?"

"The city has two faces. Like the Roman god Janus. David's words."

"Don't follow."

"You and I and everyone else see one face above the water level. A lightshow of gold and marble.

"And the other?"

"The shadowy mass of barnacled piers, sagging decks, and buckling joists that keeps the city afloat."

"Your David sounds more like a poet than an engineer."

"He's not my David, you silly man."

Over a languid meal that stretched out an hour, they talked about Zimmer's Jesus-complex and Mike's letter. "I love Zimmer's bravado and protectiveness," Tom said. "But look what happened to Gordon when he tried to run interference for us."

Chiara reached for Tom's hand. "You know, darling," she said, "that Gordon and Zimmer would not have it any other way. You're…we're…their last best hope for recovering the lost letter." She turned to smile at Giovanni who hovered near the table, ready to clear the osso bucco course. "I'm so happy that your friend Mike wrote. You know he's close enough to help if you and Zimmer need backup."

Giovanni said, "If you please, will signore and signora require anything else?"

"No, I don't think so," Tom said. "May we sit here for a while longer?"

"Of course. I bring a grappa, with my compliments."

As the waiter cleared the table of the plates, a coloratura soprano in the galley climbed the scales and painted over the clatter of pots and pans. "That is the suicide aria from Madame Butterfly" Giovanni said cheerfully. Sous-chef Roberta hopes to sing in Milano one day."

"Grappa would be great. Thanks," Tom said, giving the soupy, shredded remains of his osso bucco a last dip with a crust of bread. "So, tell me the story of your tattoo."

"A lark. Total lark. One afternoon five of us students walk into an ink parlor on the Callé Fiubera. I remember the awful smell of the place. All these antiseptic alcohols." Chiara scrunched her nose. "Wait, why are we talking about my tattoo?"

"Dunno. We've never really talked about it. Or David. Just curious. Venice coming up and all. Sooner or later," Tom said, "we should put David to rest."

"I don't like to dredge up the past. Change of topics?"

"I'd really like to know about David."

Giovanni arrived and poured glasses of grappa. "Enjoy. I leave the bottle."

"Not really your business. But if you're going to obsess over the guy, well OK." She drained her grappa and poured another for herself. "One afternoon in August we skip classes and walk along the Grand Canal. We stop at a caffé for Prosecco. I think we smoked some weed, too. David tells me that in biblical times people bonded with tattoos."

"Didn't know that."

"So, we find a tattoo shop and David draws our figure

on a scrap of paper. Two lines forming a right angle, like a half square. He tells the inker that the figure is a Daleth, the Hebrew letter 'D,' the first letter of his name in Hebrew. They argue a price, shake hands on 200 Lira, one Daleth for me, one for David."

Tom looked away from Chiara, giving her a side-glance. Her face had flushed. He should change the subject. He didn't and pressed on, feeling the effect of the wine in his head and something entirely new in his heart—a splash of jealousy. "How long were you together after Venice?"

"Back home we got engaged Thanksgiving '62, and I move into his apartment. Then I discovered he's strung out bad on heroine and violent to boot. I left him and transferred to Gonzaga in the fall of '63. Meet you Christmas '63. Rest is history."

"Do you still have feelings for David? Is that why we're not married?" Tom knew it was a cruel and absurd question. Were Chiara's feelings for this David any of his business? Hell yes. He looked at Chiara. She turned toward the window and stared out into the night. She seemed suddenly far away. He didn't know how to bring her back.

"We need to get back to Faith," Chiara said. "She's only wearing tights and a sweater and it's cold in the fast snack area."

Chapter Nine

Saint Lazarus Monastery, Venice, January 1967

Sleep didn't come that night for Chiara. She sat wide-eyed in the compartment as the train plowed through a blizzard that buried the Brenner Pass in a meter of drifting snow. Her green Tyrolean cape, a Christmas gift from Mutti, covered Tom and Faith, both sprawled across the seat, sleeping side by side. Tom snored happily. Faith's dimpled cheeks rose and fell with each breath.

The train slowed to a crawl. Outside snow sheeted against the window. A gale force wind thrashed the fir trees along the track, bending them like straws. Snow-heavy limbs snapped off with a crack that sounded like a pistol shot. Chiara's mind flung about wildly, too. She tried to read Betty Friedan and gave up. Staring into the whiteness outside, she rewound the dinner table conversation.

Tom had asked if she still had feelings for David and if she'd pulled back from his own offer of marriage because of David. The answer to the first question was No. Well, at least it was not the same depth of feeling she'd had five years earlier. You never really forget the first man you fully loved; you just put a smaller frame around the picture you carry in your heart.

The second question was edgy. She'd have to feather her thoughts more carefully. In their year as an engaged couple, she and David never set a date for a wedding. So, there was not a full arc to their story. Tom, on the other hand, even as far back as their afternoon of après ski in the Mount Spokane lodge, spoke wistfully about marriage and family. But back then the apocalypse with David still festered too much for the topic to gain traction. In the end, she and Tom worked up a little joke about the trade-off they'd reached: in lieu of a nice Catholic wedding for themselves they would celebrate a nice Catholic baptism for Faith. Chiara could still hear her mother screech and the thud of a phone on the floor when she broke the news about the family's new single mother.

Did she want to marry Tom? She wasn't sure. Just now their life felt too much like a game of Russian roulette, their chances of growing old together slimmer and slimmer the more the Sodality closed in on the family. And anyway, reading the feminists put the idea in her mind that marriage was dated and bourgeoisie. So, she'd settle for what she had. A smart, reckless, handsome lover and partner. A cherubic two-year-old daughter with a potty mouth.

At the top of the pass, the train stalled for several hours until a snowplow showed up to clear the track. Chiara's eyelids drooped. Finally, she fell asleep. When she awoke the next morning, the train, several hours late, pulled into Venice's mainland station. With Tom's help she tidied the backpacks then left their compartment to open a pneumatic exit door on the train. Stepping outside onto the ladder, she nearly lost her balance as a boot slipped on a metal foot pad.

A nearby porter caught her arm. "Welcome to Venice, Madame. Watch the step," he said, cradling her elbow and easing her onto the platform.

"*Grazie molto*, 'thanks a million'," she said to the porter when he turned to help Tom and Faith detrain and offload their backpacks.

"Have a care!" the porter said, flashing a white keyboard of teeth and touching the brim of his service hat. "Easy to lose your footing in this city of murky canals and enchanted hearts."

"Don't I know that?" Chiara muttered as she shouldered her backpack and worked her way through the foot traffic into the station. "Follow me," she said over her shoulder to Tom and Faith. "I'm heading for a gift shop that sells tickets for the *vaporetti*."

"*Vaporetti?*" Tom called after her. "What's that?"

"The water busses. Canoe-shaped steamboats that work the lagoon and canals. Our ride to the monastery." She glanced skeptically at the clouds gathering in the sky. "Let's hope it doesn't rain. The boats are open, a little wet and drafty in a storm."

"I'll wrap my anorak around Faith."

Forty-five minutes and three choppy rides later they reached the monastery on the Island of Saint Lazarus of the Armenians. Despite a rough crossing, Chiara nursed her thoughts while Faith slept. In the first boat, she told herself she'd settled the matter. It was good to revisit Venice five

67

years after she and David met there. Five years was a lot of time. No way could long ago feelings flame up and jump her firebreak. But when she boarded the second boat, she shilly-shallied. Whiffs of brackish marsh water, wails of dagger-billed loons, slanting golden light on marble buildings all pricked memories. By the third ride she felt a warmth creep up over her neck as the motorman shouted out landmarks, each one a memory recording breathless hours together with David. A first night together in the L'Imbarcadero Hotel. The Casino and a big win at a roulette table. Fizzy prosecco at the Caffè del Doge. David hijacking an empty gondola on the Rio Dei Tolentini. She clamped her eyes shut against the remembering. She could not close them tight enough.

When they reached the island's pier, a rope and pulley creaked as the boat's narrow gangway dropped onto the deck. With a loud grunt the motorman heaved their backpacks over the gunnel onto the deck. The thump, thump of their heavy luggage broke Chiara's daisy-chain of memories. She stepped gingerly down the gangway to wait for Tom and Faith as they picked their way along the wobbly plank onto the pier. Chiara placed a hand on Faith's head. It felt warm to her touch. Too warm. Oh no. She'd brought extra sweaters and shawls for Faith and a tin of suppositories against fever. Nothing else though. Maybe the monastery kitchen could provide a cup of chicken soup or even a baby aspirin for their daughter.

With a snappy salute, the motorman threw off his dock lines and chuffed away into the fog. Chiara checked her watch.

"My tummy says it's almost dinner time. Will anyone meet us here?" she asked Tom, bringing her coat tighter to her chest. "I'm cold. Help me with Faith."

Tom lifted the child into Chiara's arms then shouldered both backpacks. He said, "Do you think she's getting sick?" At the sound of a voice he turned toward the monastery.

"Hallo! Hallo, there!! Welcome to Saint Lazarus," shouted a bearded man wearing a rough wool robe and stepping briskly toward the pier. His heavy sandals beat rhythmically over the cobblestones. Heavy spectacles encased a pair of eyes set into a boney and angular face. Behind him in single file two other robed figures struggled to keep up.

"Please forgive us, dear guests," said the leader in English. "Our chapel service ran late. I am Father Vartan, abbot of the monastery. You are surely the American guests we expected. Welcome. You honor our little community by choosing to stay in our humble home." The abbot wrapped his robed arms around Tom then Chiara and blessed Faith's head with a quick sign of the cross. "You must be worn out from the trip. Our hospitality awaits you."

"Thank you," Tom said. "Yes, we're tired. But happy to arrive safely. Our daughter runs a fever though."

"Ah," the abbot said, "we'll see to her immediately. Before I forget. A telegram for you arrived yesterday. I placed it in your guest quarters. It is marked urgent."

"Telegram?" Chiara said, looking at Tom and knitting her brows in a frown. "We're not expecting any news." Tom shrugged his shoulders and shook his head.

The abbot tucked his hands into the sleeves of his robe. He introduced his two companions as Apkar and Yprad. "They are brothers," he said. "Identical twins in fact, left at the monastery gate as newborns." Both men bowed so deeply their robes crushed the dark whorls of their beards. They each reached for a backpack.

"Yprad is our guest master," the abbot explained. "And eager to offer you every kindness." He waved the brother forward.

Yprad said, "We have prepared our guest apartment for you. And a light supper."

The abbot nodded at the other brother. "Apkar is our apothecary, and even in winter he keeps a fine herb garden. What do you have for the little one's fever?"

"I recommend a pot of nettle tea and honey," Apkar said, tugging on his beard thoughtfully. "Perhaps a small glass of grappa with an aspirin. I'll help with the baggage and then prepare the medicine."

"Excellent," the abbot said. "Let's return to the monastery."

When they reached the gatehouse, the abbot threw open a wrought-iron entryway and waved his guests toward a grassy courtyard. On the far side of the gate, he held up a hand to stop the little column. "Let me officially welcome our guests to Saint Lazarus monastery," he said. "We are a prayerful but very busy community." He swept a hand across a broad quadrangle bordered on all four sides by Doric colonnades and red brick buildings.

Wisps of smoke trailed from a half dozen chimneys. Robed figures dipped in and out of the mottled light of the colonnades. "Over two centuries ago," the abbot said, "the Ottoman Turks forced us from our beloved Armenia. But thanks to the grace of God the doge of Venice settled us here in a life of prayer and service. In former times, the island housed a leper colony." He snuck a glance at his visitors, who cringed at this mention. He always enjoyed the look on his guests' face when he mentioned the colony.

The abbot waved his entourage on, crossing the quadrangle and pausing at a circular stone wall. "Our very own well and source of fresh water for the community and our pear and apple trees." Without a word, the abbot ducked into a covered walkway and dropped out of sight. "This way, please," he called out from the shadows.

"To the right," Abkar told Tom and Chiara, as they looked around for their host.

"Over here," shouted the abbot. They found him in front of a padlocked and bolted steel door, jingling a set of keys on a ring. He picked one to open the lock. Throwing the bolt, he stepped into a dim foyer and climbed a spiral staircase that led to a hallway.

At the end of the hall the abbot produced an iron ring from inside his wide sleeve and fumbled with more keys. He unlocked the door, swung it wide, and stepped back. Chiara and Tom both sucked in their breath at the same time. "Is something wrong?" the abbot said, watching their eyes go wide with shock.

"Wrong?" Chiara said, "It's heavenly. She and Tom turned in a full circle, taking in an elegant, high-ceilinged suite of rooms with a view of Venice's lagoon. Outside speedboats and taxis threaded the water, lacing the surface

71

with frothy wakes. "Is that Saint Mark's Cathedral?" Tom asked the abbot, pointing to a glittering dome on the Venice skyline. The abbot said it was.

"Thank you for such lovely quarters," Chiara said. "Look at this, Tom." She ran a hand over a divan whose brocaded fabric was shot with gold accents. She pulled Tom toward a group of Empire chairs and a cherry wood divan, sighing audibly. "Mother loves Damask silk and patterns of botanical figures. Not so much Kernan rugs." Kicking off her boots she walked to a cast bronze crucifix on one wall. She ran a finger over the figure of Christ on the cross.

The abbot said, "Bernini. Or at least his school."

"Bernini," Chiara said, reverently. "Bernini." Chiara genuflected and crossed herself. "Haven't done that since convent school."

"Ah," the abbot said, "you know our Italian masters. Now look at your sleeping room." He opened a paneled door. With a swell of pride in his voice he said, "Brother Michael, our carpenter, just installed your bed. It is a masterpiece, don't you think? He turned the burled walnut panels of an old confessional booth into your footboard and headboard."

"Wow," Tom said, looking at Chiara. "Quite a change from a Marquette walk-up furnished with early St. Vincent de Paul."

"We leave you now," the abbot said, waving the two young monks out of the room.

"Wait," Tom said. "You mentioned a telegram."

"Oh, yes, of course. Forgive me. It's there on the

nightstand next to the bed. Oh, and another thing. Your friend Sona Routanian sent you a message. She is safe. As you know, her uncle is the monastery's librarian. His name is Father Samvel.

"Safe?" Chiara said. "Thank God."

"Quite safe," the abbot said. "An Armenian community in another city took in the Routanians and their children. More I cannot say."

Chapter Ten

Venice, January 1967

As the door clicked shut behind the monks, Chiara opened Gordon's telegram and read the message out loud to Tom. "MY RECOVERY SLOW. AM NOW IN SECURE HOSPITAL. GOD SPEED. DR. GORDON."

"Secure hospital?" Tom said, crunching his eyebrows. "Where would that be?"

"God only knows," Chiara sighed. "At least Sona and the children are safe. We should telegram that news to Gordon. Except we have no idea where he is. God, I feel like we've thrown our friends overboard. Joseph, Precious, Gordon, Sona." She folded the telegram and dropped it on a side table.

Ten minutes later there was a tap on the door. Opening it, she stood aside for Apkar who rolled in a dinner cart laden with food and a tray of remedies for Faith. "With the compliments of the abbot," he said. "Here is a pitcher of Veneto red. On the serving dishes you'll find a first course of pasta puttanesca and a second course of thin-sliced roast ham and squid boiled in its own ink. The baskets hold fruits of the season from Sicily. Enjoy. Oh, and another thing. Tonight there is a gala near St Mark's Cathedral. Music and fireworks."

When the door closed behind Apkar, they set fatigue and worry aside for the moment to savor their first full meal in over two days. Throwing wide the bedroom drapes Chiara pillowed up her family in bed. As they ate, the festival on the mainland exploded into the night with red starbursts and white comets colorizing the sky over Saint Mark's Square. And then, when a vial of herbal medication and a tablespoon of grappa put Faith to sleep, they made love—leisurely and wantonly.

The next morning a balled fist banged on the apartment door. Tom didn't move so Chiara sat up and muffled a yawn. With a slow roll she turned toward Tom and placed a foot on the small of his back. She pushed him toward the edge of the bed. "Answer the door. Pa—leeese. Before my head splits open. Stop! You're missing your pajama bottoms. Put a bathrobe on."

In the courtyard outside, a chapel bell pealed two short tones for the half hour, nine deep ones for the hour. Chiara did the math. Damn. 9:30 a.m. For sure, they'd missed breakfast in the refectory. So much for an early start on her walking tour of Venice this morning. "So, who is it?"

"Yprad, the guest master," Tom called from the hallway. "We've overslept. He brought up a food tray. I'll put it on the kitchen table."

After a flurry of snatching food, dressing Faith, and fine-tuning plans, Chiara followed Tom and Faith out of the apartment and locked the apartment door. At the pier she tightened Faith's neck scarf then gave Tom a last hug and kiss. She hiked Faith over the dock lines that snugged two sleek water taxis—one emerald green, one periwinkle blue—to deck cleats.

A motorman in a pea jacket and knit cap waved Chiara and Faith aboard the green boat and settled them into a warm cabin. As the boat eased away from the pier Chiara waved and blew kisses at Tom. Out of the corner of her eye she caught a glimpse of a woman in a red coat inside the other water taxi. Huh. Who was that? Another guest on their floor? They could have shared a taxi.

Tom blew kisses to Faith and Chiara as the water taxi put the pier to stern and sliced into the ground fog. Then, when there was only the muffled ring-ding of its two-cylinder engine on the lagoon, he turned to look at the other taxi tied up at the pier. Must be a local dignitary visiting the monastery. Or one of the monks with an errand in the city. A moment later that boat chuffed off into the fog, too.

He turned around to walk back to the monastery with his mind tossing back and forth between one niggling thought and another. He fretted about Chiara's walking tour. She knew the city well enough. But Faith looked peaky. And then there was Dr. Gordon still in a hospital. Not to mention Sona and her family in hiding.

In a simpler world he should feel giddy about having the *Panarion* close to hand. Instead, he could only see the trail of violence they'd left behind in Milwaukee. He stared at his wristwatch for a long minute. Its hands seemed sluggish, unwilling to chop off pieces of time. The day, drawn out with anxiety rather than work, would not go by swiftly.

Now late for his appointment with Father Samvel, he fast walked across the quadrangle. Reaching the door to their building, he vaulted up the staircase two steps at a time to collect his briefcase and notes. He nearly collided with Father Vartan and another monk.

"Good morning, Tom," the abbot said, "I hope the breakfast was satisfactory."

"Thanks for the courtesy of room service. We overslept."

The abbot said, "May I introduce you to our librarian, Father Samvel? He is the uncle of your friend Sona Routanian."

Tom offered his hand. "Pleased to finally meet you, Father Samvel," he said. "Chiara and I are so happy that Sona is safe."

"We all are," Father Samvel said, holding out a delicate, ink-stained hand. "I'm also the monastery's calligrapher," he explained. "Keeping nibs, brushes, and ink in order is a dirty business," he said with a chuckle. He was a tall man, well over six feet. There were holes in the elbows of his robe, frayed, Tom guessed, from long hours bent over his inkpots.

Tom fell in behind the two monks as they walked down the hall and turned into a curious room, a warren of books, fine furniture, and two mummies. "Lord Byron's Room," the abbot said without any explanation. At the far end of the room the three men entered a pass-through airlock that sealed off the library from the rest of the building. On the other side of the airlock, they stepped through a second door onto a landing that looked upwards into the library's vaulted ceiling and downwards into a rotunda two floors below. A whoosh of cool, dry air tickled Tom's ears. "The library must have a huge HVAC unit," he said with a full-body shiver and a mental note to bring a heavier sweater next time.

"The younger monks joke and call it our iron lung," the abbot said, crossing the landing to a nautilus staircase that spiraled down to the library stacks and reading tables.

Tom looked down into an architectural wonder. A parquet floor gleamed with geometric designs. Glass-fronted bookcases, nearly two floors high, ringed the circular wall of the rotunda. He looked up. Above him fanned out a wood-framed dome, arcing seventy-five feet from the ground floor. A cone of polished pinewood slats hung from the dome. "What a —."

"Tom, I leave you here with Father Samvel," the abbot said. "I must return to the community." He whispered something to the librarian that Tom did not catch. A moment later the air lock hissed and closed behind the abbot.

Chapter Eleven

Venice, January 1967

As Chiara's water taxi chugged across a choppy lagoon, Faith whimpered, "Head hurt, Mama." Chiara put a hand to the child's face. Damn. Warm again. Mercifully not hot. Somewhere in his apothecary Apkar had found a sachet of chewable aspirin. Chiara reached for a tablet and pressed one between Faith's lips.

A half hour later, the taxi tied up at a private dock near the ferry terminal San Marco. After the motorman helped them both off the boat, they walked hand in hand toward the *Calle Vallaresso*, a broad street that led to Saint Mark's Cathedral Square. "I know a special restaurant where we can find lunch," Chiara told Faith. "And have an ice cream cone." By the time they reached the Cathedral, the campanile bell struck 11:00 a.m. Faith's cheeks looked even more flushed, and Chiara decided to skip a tour of Saint Mark's and find her restaurant.

At the Grand Canal they cut through the late morning foot traffic on the deck of the Rialto Bridge. "Not much longer, my darling," Chiara told Faith, as they stopped at a pushcart in the bridge arcade to try on silk scarves.

"Pretties," Faith said. "Want one."

"Of course, you do, darling," Chiara said, happy to see Faith perk up. She sorted through a leafy cloud of silk scarves on a rack. There was give and take over the price, hesitation, doubt, and finally a deal. As they left the bridge, Chiara looked back. A bright red smudge of color in a blue water taxi on the far side of the Canal caught her eye. Huh, was that the boat from the monastery? Nah. Venice was a city of a thousand blue boats and red coats.

Chiara carried Faith along the Grand Canal, walking briskly down the busy *Riva del Vin*. When they reached its intersection with the *Calle dei Cinque* she swung right. Here was a neighborhood she'd known so well. She picked up her pace. Nothing seemed to have changed. Shuttered apartments. Mesh works of laundry lines and wrought-iron balconies. Here a cast iron brazier set up against a storefront. There a policeman sitting on a nail keg, playing chess with a villainous looking seaman. "Sorry," she muttered, easing Faith around the brazier and working her way past oily windows full of elaborate tea sets, wax and feather flower arrangements, decorated eggshells.

She stopped to gather her thoughts. This morning the *Calle* looked tired and forlorn, a haven for slackers and knickknacks and curios. Maybe it was always so. But back in the day she thought it more like a home to spirited merchants, designer clothing, jewelry, antiques, a street of grandeur, style, romance. Well, of course that had been five years ago. She'd fallen wooly-headed in love with David, hadn't she? And love, she'd learned the hard way was a trick lens that lied about its subjects.

Chiara put Faith down and grabbed her hand. Side by side they made their way down the street. Suddenly, she stopped. Her heart rate notched up. Not ten meters away a fretted light slanted through the windows of the Caffè del Doge. She tugged on Faith, and they stepped up to the window. With her coat sleeve she wiped away the pearls of water beading down a pane and peered inside.

There was the round bistro table where she and David spent long afternoons. Memories rose like a tide in her mind. Nothing had changed inside. Against one wall, the coffee bar glittered with polished mirrors, stainless steel beer taps, and brass expresso machines. Even the curly, twisted pastries in the two glass-faced cupboards felt like old friends. She scooped up Faith and carried her into the Caffè, easing her onto one of the fan-backed chairs. Gosh even the cracked vinyl seat cushion still pinched the back of her legs as she removed her coat and sat down. She drank in the moment, rewinding her life back five years. Easier than she'd thought.

A waitress stepped up with a booster chair. Chiara said, "Hot chocolate and a croissant for my daughter, a cappuccino and a ham panini for me." As they waited for the order, Faith doodled on a napkin with crayons from Chiara's shoulder bag.

An alphabet soup of gouged-out initials pitted the tabletop. Chiara's fingers glided over the letters as if they were a Ouija-board, settling finally on a faint DK and CO. She laughed at herself. What did she expect the carvings to tell her? She never found out. Faith's box of crayons clattered onto the floor. Chiara bent over to pick them up. She saw a pair of men's shoes planted at their table. She looked up into the face of a waiter who peered at her through wire spectacles.

He said, "Can it be you, Miss Chiara, the beautiful American lady who stayed at the Palazzo Dario five years ago?" His nostrils flared like the gills of a fish, and he spoke a fine, if nasal English.

Chiara nodded. Her face reddened. She hadn't banked on being recognized after so many years. Now what?

"You have come back to us! Do you remember me? I am Giancarlo. Who can forget your flashing smile? You arrived at my table every day as regular as the morning star. I called you Venus."

"Of course, I remember you, dear Giancarlo." Chiara laughed and stood, hugging the old man's bony shoulders. His face came back to her with clarity. Hair matted around his temples, tufts poking out from behind each ear. His smell, too. Yeast dough and warm crusty bread. "You always painted a rose on our cappuccinos." Chiara nudged Faith. "Say hello to this nice man."

"Hello. Me Faith."

The waiter pressed a chocolate into her palm.

"You and Mr. David have a child and now come back to Venice?" It was more a statement of fact than a question. His eyes twinkled. He spoke with lightness and honest remembering.

Before Chiara could answer, a door opened. A sudden draft of cold air swept over her table. She shuddered but didn't know why.

From the pier at the Rialto Bridge all the way to the Caffè, Mira Borja had shadowed Chiara and Faith. She kept a good distance behind them until she reached the restaurant. Through the window she saw Chiara speak to a waiter who handed the child a chocolate. When she made her entrance, she flung the door wide and held it open so that a stream of cold air swept through the opening. She hoped Chiara felt her presence before she saw her. Chiara didn't look up.

She glided up to Chiara's table, eager to pop up out of nowhere, a wraith riding in on an air current. She simpered softly as Chiara started, looked up then caught her breath in disbelief. Lovely how the woman ran her eyes admiringly over the red Olivela coat. Even more delicious to watch Chiara's mouth pinch into a thin smile. Mira could almost hear the gears in Chiara's head working. She held out a gloved hand then pulled it back when Chiara let it dangle in the air.

Without waiting for an invitation Mira unbuckled her coat. She pulled off her gloves, dropped them on the table, and ordered Giancarlo to bring a chair.

Faith reached across the table and grabbed Chiara's hand. "Hold me, Mama," she said.

"Faith, don't you remember me?" Mira said, reaching to pinch the child's cheek. Faith pulled back. "Well, running into you two in Venice? In a restaurant? How is it even possible? What a small world!"

"Right," Chiara answered. "Who knew it was this small?"

"I think I'll order a café latte. Will you have one with

me?"

"No thank you. We're just leaving. Faith has a fever."

"What are you and your daughter doing in Venice this time of year?"

"Er...ah...my parents gave us an Italian holiday for Christmas."

Well, she thinks fast on her feet. Dodging my question. She pressed on. "You're traveling without Tom?" She tutted theatrically, hoping she sounded shocked and surprised. It felt good to dig at this bitch. Of course, she knew Tom was in Venice, too.

"No. Tom's here."

"Wonderful. Where are you staying? We should arrange to meet. I'd love to see Tom."

"I'm sure you would," Chiara said. "With a local religious community that my parents support."

"But where exactly?" Mira asked. She loved playing cat and mouse with the woman. "In one of the luxury hotels on the Grand Canal?" Her voice oozed sarcasm. She knew exactly where they stayed. Down the hall from her apartment in the monastery's guest quarters.

"At the Armenian monastery on the island of San Lazaro."

"Oh my God," Mira said, pressing a hand to her chest and dropping her jaw. "Me, too." Lovely how Chiara's face knotted and how her hand crumpled the cloth napkin on her lap. "The monastery holds family property in trust. I'm here to have it reappraised."

"Family?" Chiara repeated.

"You're so silly, Chiara. Surely, I've told you and

Tom. My surname is Borja, the Spanish side of the famous Borgias. Lucretia Borgia. Caesar Borgia. Pope Alexander IV.

"Famous?" Chiara said. "Right. For greed, murder, lust. Present company excepted, I'm sure."

Ewe. The woman had a bite. "Sure about a coffee?"

"Yes. You'll have to excuse us. Faith's running a fever and I need to give her an aspirin."

"How…how…maternal of you. See you for dinner at the monastery? Do bring Tom."

Chapter Twelve

Venice, January 1967

The hissing of the library's airlock made Tom feel even more cut off from Chiara and Faith. He couldn't shake off his worry about the plan to visit the city with a sick child. "Mind the steps," Father Samvel said, cutting into Tom's thoughts and hiking his robe to keep from tripping on the hem.

At the bottom of the staircase the librarian strode toward two tables and stopped at the one holding a supply of cotton gloves. He withdrew a pair for himself and a pair for Tom. "If you please. We take every care to protect our rare books."

Settling his guest at the second table, he sat across from Tom. On the table between the two men rested an X-form cradle, its air cushions supporting the *Panarion*. The 1500-year-old codex lay open to a center page. It looked more fragile than Tom remembered. With his shirtsleeve he swiped at beads of perspiration on his forehead.

Leaning over the cradle Father Samvel poked the air cushions with his right forefinger. "Just making sure the pressure is high enough to prevent the book from opening too wide and damaging the spine."

As Tom touched the cradle's arms with his gloved hands, he felt a jolt of excitement run up his arms. Dude. He felt jazzed. Buzzed. Out-of-body. Whatever. Flicking on a conservator's lamp, he watched the dun color of the vellum warm to near yellow in the soft light. Now brightened, the pages showed their age: cracks and ridges in the vellum ran in every direction. Even stressed and tired, the Armenian script was still clear and readable. He thought about Sona Routanian and her joy at holding the book in her hands. And the terrible price she'd paid for doing so.

Tom grabbed his briefcase and pulled out his notebook, magnifying glass, caliper, and face mask. "It's time," he said to Samvel, slipping the mask over his mouth. Father Samvel stood up and with infinite care opened the codex to the last three folios. Tom's heart pumped faster as he stared at words written down at the same time as the Roman Empire crumbled. He fought back the urge to touch the Armenian version of the Laodicean Letter.

Tom stood up and leaned over the codex. "I noticed this back in Milwaukee. And it still bugs me. The Letter, what I call the Androgyne Papyrus, only covers the front side of the last three pages. The back sides are blank. Why was that?"

"I don't know," the librarian said with a shrug of his shoulders. "Perhaps the translator or his scribe planned to add some commentary on the text on the back side?"

Tom shook his head. Didn't buy it. He'd come back to

the blank pages later. He pulled Sona's English translation of the Letter from his briefcase. He read the first line. *"In Christ Jesus there is neither Jew nor Greek, slave nor free, male nor female."* He looked up at Samvel. "That's from Apostle Paul's Letter to the Galatians."

"I know the verse," the librarian said. "Our younger monks think it reason enough to invite women to join our monastery community." He shook his head, grimly.

"I have another question for you." What do you think happened to the Greek original after the Armenian translator copied his version onto these last three pages?"

"The Greek original? Probably went into a geniza or storeroom for ancient manuscripts. Over time the papyrus fibers rotted."

"But that doesn't make sense. The Letter was...is an authentic writing of Apostle Paul."

"Yes, but one that Holy Mother Church didn't keep in the New Testament."

Hmm. Tom changed the subject again. "To be honest I'm only here for a forensic look at these three leaves. Not to argue theology."

"Forensic? I don't follow."

"I'd like to measure the thickness of the pages, for example."

"Of course," Samvel said. "Funny thing, you're the first person to pay any notice to the blank sides."

"Well, I've thought about them a lot. My hunch is that the last three leaves are really envelope pages protecting something inside."

"You speak in puzzles to me, I fear. Envelope pages?"

Father Samvel shuffled his feet uncomfortably and picked at the frayed cloth on his sleeve.

"If I'm right those pages can tell us where to find the original Greek Letter," Tom said. He paused then threw caution to the wind. "Look. You recall that one of the pages had an enigma riddle on the margin. Something like: 'two equals three and three equals two. What am I'?"

"Yes, I remember. A little brain teaser. You have a solution?"

"Maybe one that accounts for the blank sides and the extra thickness. What if 'three equals two' means that the three envelopes contain two writings—the Armenian version of the Letter on the front pages and the original Greek Letter inside the three envelopes?"

"And the other part of the riddle?"

"'Two equals three' means two leaves each for the three envelopes."

"Ingenious young man," the librarian said as he looked at this wristwatch. "But we'll never know. To prove your theory you would have to destroy the pages." He glanced at his watch. "Oh, dear God. I'm late for prayers. I leave you now and let you find your way out. Later, I'll return the codex to our vaults."

Chapter Thirteen

Tom watched the curator leave the library and climb the staircase. Thank God. On the verge of a pulse-pounding discovery he needed time alone with the *Panarion* and its three envelope pages. Settling back in his chair, he flipped through his notebook to the pages he and Gordon filled when they examined the book at Marquette. The notes detailed the heavy wear, insect larvae, and mold damage to all the pages except the last three. Those three, Gordon wrote down—more as a guess than a finding—were better preserved because they were newer. Tom looked next at Gordon's crude, hand-ruler measurements of the envelopes' dimensions. Their length and width matched the other leaves in the book. However, they were thicker than the other pages by an average of one sixteenth of an inch.

Tom turned to Gordon's notes on the condition of the book's vellum, or better, its vellums. Under his magnifying glass Gordon had determined that calfskin vellum—with its full grain and clear tone—made up all the leaves of the book save the last three. Those were goatskin vellum—cloudier in tone and creamier across the grain.

Tom put the notebook down and reached for the caliper. Calibrated to one thirty-second of an inch, it measured with scientific precision. He tested for thickness every two inches on all sides of the last three pages, recording his data. For comparison's sake he measured random leaves from inside the book. Then he averaged the findings.

The results jumped out. He gave a loud whoop. The last three pages were always thicker by almost an eighth of an inch than the rest of the pages in the book.

Now only one more set of observations to make. With his magnifying glass he began to look for evidence of stitches holding the outer edges of the envelopes together. At first Tom could find no trace of a seam. In his notebook, he jotted down his conclusion—most likely time and wear crushed the edges of the vellum together and bonded their fibers to the stitchery. Tucking his glass back into his shoulder bag, his fingers grasped a small vial. It was Chiara's bottle of nail polish remover that she'd loaned him to clean up his calipers.

Wait. What if he smeared a drop of the acetone on a page corner and waited to see if the vellum and the thread reacted differently, say pulled apart, or changed color? If the thread were silk, it might just work. Seracin, the outer gum covering of silk thread was soluble, and might present itself differently from the water-resistant goat skin vellum of the envelopes. Not exactly science. And probably a violation of library policy. Not probably. For sure a violation. Still, he might not get a second chance to test his theory.

Tom drizzled a bead of liquid from the vial onto the upper right corner of the first envelope. With the point of his caliper he worked the bead into the vellum. A minute passed by. Then two. The vellum didn't react to the strong solvent. There was nothing and then suddenly there was something—a barely visible line of thread formed along the edge of the page. With his lens Tom magnified the area. Hallelujah. Fine threading wound its way around the corner of the page, stitching it together. Riddle resolved. Two became three and three became two. He pulled a 35 mm Leica from his shoulder bag, adjusted the lighting from the lamp, and shot several frames of the pages.

Had he found the Androgyne Papyrus, or what was left of it? He couldn't yet be sure. In the morning he'd ask a huge favor of the abbot. Would he allow the librarian or conservator to surgically open the envelope pages?

Tom stood up, shouldered his bag, and then looked for a long moment at the cradled codex. He batted away a niggling feeling, almost a worry, about the book's safety. Put the thought aside. Father Samvel promised to return and take the book back to its vault. Nothing to be gained by hanging out in the library.

Ten minutes later he walked through the door to their apartment. There was sizzling news to tell Chiara. "Anyone home?"

"In here," Chiara said as the door to the apartment clicked shut. She heard footfalls in the carpeted hallway that led to the bedroom. She set aside the cool cloth she'd applied to Faith's forehead. On the nightstand next to the

95

bed a rectal thermometer read 101. Chiara kissed the child's pink cheek. The skin felt hot on her lips. Still sleeping, Faith burbled a soft sound.

She sighed. It'd been a gamble to bring a sick child to Venice. She'd lost, and now it was pell mell back to Göttingen, to Mutti, who'd find a proper doctor to care for Faith. Meanwhile, Tom had news to share, and she was eager to hear what he'd discovered in the library. Afterwards, she'd tell him about meeting Mira Borja. She rubbed a knuckle across her cheeks, leaving a tawny swath of eyeliner and rouge on her face. Her hand brushed over the crown of her head. Yikes. Time for a haircut before she grew a riotous pouf. How long had she and Faith slept? She looked at the clock. Well over an hour.

Tom walked in and flung his coat on the bed. There was still enough daylight streaming through the drapes to show a grin edging across his face. She stood up, threw her arms around his neck, and kissed him. "Hi, darling. Faith's sleeping. Better not turn the light on."

"OK. How is she? Still feverish? You guys just get back?"

"Shhhh. You'll wake Faith. No. Couple of hours ago. I don't think the fever's spiking."

Tom leaned and kissed the little hand that poked out from the blanket. "Stay healthy, little one. We've got lotsa work to do."

"Tell me about your day," Chiara whispered." She pointed toward the sitting room. "Out there so we don't wake up Faith." Chiara reached for Tom's hand, and they tiptoed out of the room.

In the sitting room Tom filled two glasses with the remnant of the Veneto red. He sat next to Chiara on the brocaded divan. "Well, to use technical terms: Bull's eye, bingo, the whole kielbasa," he said, laughing and hugging Chiara. He pulled his black notebook from the briefcase and said, "I've got it all recorded in here. I know where Apostle Paul's original Letter is. We've found the Androgyne Papyrus! Tomorrow you and I meet with the librarian." Words tumbled out like gumballs from a jimmied dispenser as he went over his morning in the library.

Chiara held up a hand. "Slow down. That's great. Tell me more. One spoonful of good news at a time."

"Don't know where to start. The library will amaze you, it's so cool." He told about the airlock, the two-story high bookcases, the spiral staircase, a great cone hanging from a vaulted ceiling. He paused to draw a breath then described the cradle that held the book, then the *Panarion* itself. "It was all I could do to hold back from ripping to the last pages of the book and taking my measurements. But first I asked Father Samvel about the blank verso sides of the last three pages. And that's when things got a little strange."

"Verso?"

"Back side of a page. Anyway, Samvel claimed he hadn't noticed the blank sides until that morning."

Chiara shook her head. She picked up her glass and drained it. "That's impossible. He sent the book to you and Gordon at Marquette."

Tom said, "Gets stranger. I give him our solution to

the riddle; say it means that the last three folios are envelope pages that protect what's left of the Letter. He blows me off and says he needs to leave. So, I do what I came to do, a little forensic work with my caliper."

"Sorry about the way Samvel acted. Still, you seem really pleased with something," Chiara said, reaching for the notebook and flipping slowly through its coded pages.

"Well, I worked it out: the final three pages are thicker than the rest of the leaves in the book. And I'm convinced that they are envelopes that hide something. I found evidence of stitching."

"Now what?"

"Gets a little sticky now. Tomorrow you and I meet with Father Davit, the library's conservator. Ask him to open up the envelopes and remove their contents."

"You're kidding? Father Vartan and Father Samvel will agree?"

"Anyone's guess. Stand by for more excitement tomorrow."

Chiara stood up and walked into the bedroom. "Just checking on Faith," she said over her shoulder. She returned a moment later. "Still sleeping. Breathing sounds normal."

"So how did your day in Venice go?"

Chiara reached for her empty glass. "I could use another glass of Veneto red. I had my share of excitement, too," Chiara said, her voice worn and flat. "And I think I'm going to disappoint you."

"What's the matter?" Tom put a hand on Chiara's shoulder.

"Just a head's up. If the fever spikes. I think I'll leave tomorrow. Mutti will know a baby doctor."

"Fingers crossed. I'm counting on you to work with me in the conservatory. Record and witness what we find. I can't trust anyone else."

"And I want that more than anything, too. Unless Faith gets sicker." Chiara stood up to open a window. A sea breeze rustled the heavy drapes against her face. On the lagoon, the red and green running lights of watercraft flecked the surface. High over the city hung a halo of incandescent mist. Tom's findings in the library thrilled her. Truly. And she longed to be part of his discoveries tomorrow. But things had gotten tangled. Faith's rising fever. The shocking visit from Mira in the Caffè. Conjuring up David. She closed the window and turned to face Tom, who eased up behind her and put his arms around her waist.

"This morning Mira Borja showed up out of nowhere," Chiara said. "At the Caffè del Doge. She walked in like she owned the place and plunked herself at our table."

"Caffè del Doge?"

"Yes, Mira. David and I used to hang out there. I was there tripping on nostalgia."

"Whoa! You went back to David's favorite Caffè and Mira showed up. I don't know where to start asking questions. David I get. But Mira? What the hell is she doing here? You sure? Mira? Mira Borja?"

"Get this. She's a guest here in the monastery, too. I'm pretty sure she followed us into the city in the other water taxi we saw this morning at the pier. Says she's got relatives in Venice. Patrons of the monastery. Claims she's here to check on some family property that the abbot holds in trust." As she talked about the encounter with Mira, a heaviness grew in her chest.

"Tom, listen to me, carefully," Chiara said. "That woman damn well knew we were in Venice and staying here."

"Knew we were in Venice? No way. No one knew that except Gordon and Zimmer. Joseph and FBI Agent Shay, too, I guess. What'd she want?"

"To warn us off, maybe? I don't know. To confirm that we were in Venice. To find out about you. I think someone in the monastery told her we were here."

"Find out about me?" Tom said. "Why me?"

Why him? God, men can be so thick. "Well, your research, I guess." And a little man-conquest on the side. Not a guess.

"Project?" Tom, said with a short laugh. "That's silly. Mira's just a foreign student with a shady family. What does she know about my work? Or even care? You don't think...No, it couldn't be."

"Look, I'm sorry to muddy things for you just now," Chiara said. "I know you need me. But I just don't have the strength to deal with Mira, the Project, and maybe a sick child. Of course, I'll stay if Faith feels better in the morning. But just in case, please be ready to carry on without us. Why don't you arrange for a water taxi tonight to stand by at the pier tomorrow?"

Chapter Fourteen

Venice, January 1967

Tom ordered the water taxi then jumped up at a knock on the door. "Come in, please," he called. "It's Yprad," he said over his shoulder to Chiara. "I ordered some dinner for us."

The guest master wheeled a dinner cart into the room. He lifted the lid on a steaming cast iron pot. "The kitchen prepared minestrone soup." He removed the covers from two heavy platters and a soup tureen. "There are some sandwiches, and a fruit plate. In a bowl some pudding for the child." From under his robe he brought out a bottle of grappa and winked. "The abbot's personal stock. And something for the child. More yarrow tea and petals of wildflower." Chiara looked at Tom and rolled her eyes. As the monk turned to leave, he tapped the side of his head with a fist. "Oh yes, the abbot reminds Tom about his appointment tomorrow morning with Father Davit, our conservator. 9 a.m."

The next morning, Tom helped Chiara dress Faith in warm leggings and a heavy sweater. The child's fever was gone. "Not bad for a medieval pharmacy," Tom said.

He got an elbow jab in the ribs from Chiara. Hand in hand they crossed the quadrangle toward the refectory. Pausing at the well, Tom gave Faith a small coin. "Make a wish and throw the coin down the well," he said.

"OK," Faith said, dropping the coin in the well. "Mama and Faith stay here with Papa."

"I wish," Tom said, tenderly.

In the refectory they found the monks bent over their porridge, yogurt, and black bread. A cloud of cigarette smoke and a low rumble of conversation hung in the air. With its long oak tables, high-backed chairs, and tapestries of battle scenes the space seemed more a war room than a dining hall. At the head table sat the abbot and the librarian, smoking their pipes. Tom pointed to a table marked *Visitors* and seated his family.

When breakfast arrived, Tom and Chiara spooned up their porridge and took turns wiping bits of the gruel from Faith's chin. Tom reached for a plate of black bread and a jar of butter, offering a slice to Chiara who shook her head. They ate in silence until Tom asked Chiara, "I guess I should wave off the water taxi, right?" Before Chiara could answer, a young monk, breathless from running, entered the refectory. He approached Tom. "Sir," he said breathlessly, "This just arrived. Marked Urgent."

Tom ripped open a telegram envelope, read silently, and handed the envelope to Chiara. "It's from Mutti. My God, someone broke into our apartment in Göttingen and trashed all the rooms. Mutti begs us to come home immediately." Questions flooded his mind. Who broke in? Why? Neighbors hear anything? Were the police already on the scene? They had to leave immediately. What rotten luck. How could this happen just when he had the Androgyne Papyrus within his grasp. "This is a nightmare," he said, showing Chiara the telegram. "I can't leave. I may not get another chance to work on the *Panarion.*"

Chiara read the message and clapped a hand to her forehead. "Oh my God. Oh my God. Yes, No. What am I trying to say?"

"Darling, I need to put you and Faith on the next express train for home. I'll help you pack. I'll follow tomorrow or the next day at the latest."

"You're right. You're right," Chiara said. Let's eat a decent breakfast together first."

"Oh shit. Now this," Tom said as he looked up from the table and saw Mira Borja standing in the entrance to the refectory.

Mira hovered for a moment in the doorway then sauntered toward Tom and Chiara's table. They looked stressed as they bent over their food, talking earnestly about something or other. Maybe an argument? Sweet. She filed the thought for later use. Yesterday at the Caffè she'd fallen flat on her face because Chiara had abruptly walked off with the child. This morning she'd dressed to kill, choosing calf-hugging, high heeled boots, tailored gaucho pants, and a lamb's wool jacket. When she saw Chiara hand the child a slice of bread and jam, she moved in. Putting extra weight on her spiked heels, she clicked the metal taps sharply on the flagstone floor. Chiara wheeled around to look, and the bread and jam fell from her hand onto the table.

With long, leggy strides Mira covered the distance from the doorway to the table where the monks ate. "May one of your patronesses join you men?" she said. A dozen cowled heads swiveled, froze, and then turned back to porridge bowls, spooning up the gruel furiously. She nudged the abbot and the librarian, squeezing between them into the open bench space. Before chatting up the Americans, she'd vamp these men without women and send them running to confession with minds full of naughty ideas.

After a short conversation with the abbot Mira excused herself and glided over to the Americans' table. With practiced courtesy she kissed all three of them on the cheek. "Missed the three of you at dinner last night," she said to Chiara. Without waiting for an answer, she draped a hand over Tom's shoulder, "Tom, did Chiara tell you we met at the Caffè del Doge? Such serendipity!"

"Mira's hand lingered on Tom's shoulder. He moved closer to Chiara, and Mira wedged herself in next to Tom.

"Well, Mir-ra," Chiara said, stretching out the name like a rubber band, "I just heard you speaking a very fluent Italian with the monks at the other table. You're keeping secrets from us."

"It's my mother tongue, silly," Mira said with a flick of a wrist. She bristled at the tone in Chiara's voice. The woman needed a good slap across the face.

"I'm curious. Why did you leave Marquette and come to Venice, to this monastery?" Chiara asked. She loaded a slice of bread with jam and took a savage bite.

"Not that it's any of your business, Chiara," Mira said. "I told you yesterday the abbot holds my family assets in

104

trust. I needed to get some jewelry and artwork reappraised." She forced a smile. Nosey bitch. Careful now. Play nice. You're here to find out what Tom's up to in the monastery.

"Surely you have a local agent who could handle an appraisal for you," Tom said.

"I'm a—how do you Americans say it?—a hands-on-person and…"

"Your latte, Contessa," said the waiter, holding out a cup and saucer.

Mira took a sip. It was delicious. But she needed to go on offence and stop feeling defensive. She barked at the waiter. "This is dishwater. Bring me some orange juice." Time to change the subject.

"So, Tom, how are your studies going? You still on some old project with Professor Gordon? Is that what brought you here?"

"Same project. New phase. Working on my thesis in Germany. Early Christian anthologies of Bible texts. Some interesting examples here in the monastery's holdings. Working with the conservator in the library."

Mira leaned into Tom. "I'd love to know more."

Chiara pushed her chair away from the table as if to leave. "You'll have to excuse us, Mira. I'm in a bit of a rush this morning."

"Sorry to rush off," Tom said. "I want to help the girls pack. They're leaving on the afternoon express train for home. Someone burgled our apartment."

"I'm sorry to hear that," Mira said, squeezing a note of sympathy into her voice as the seed of a plan sprouted in her head.

"Mama and Faith go on train," Faith said. "Bad man hurt my toys."

Mira squeezed a note of sympathy into her voice. "Travel well, ladies. I'm sure Tom will miss you. Excuse me. I must speak with the abbot. I'm sure Tom will find plenty to do here in the monastery." She fairly skated out of the refectory at this chance opening into Tom's project.

After Tom helped the girls pack, he hoisted Faith on his shoulders with a cheerful "Upsadaisyum." He and Chiara cut across the quadrangle lawn, passed under the gatehouse arch, and made for the pier. Behind them Yprad and Apkar padded along, carrying the backpacks and a woven basket of panini and fruit. In an act of kindness, the abbot had arranged for Yprad to accompany Chiara and Faith as far as the Austrian border.

Tom looked up at the few high clouds scudding across the sky. The weather looked bright, the lagoon flat. Smooth crossing for Chiara and Faith. Though he'd arranged for first class train tickets, there were long layovers in Salzburg and Munich. He felt awful sending the girls home alone. He'd make it up to them in spades.

A motorman emerged from the water taxi's engine compartment, waving his passengers onboard with an oily rag in his hand. Tom put Faith on the deck and kissed her good-bye. She wrapped her arms around his neck. "Miss you, Papa." He hugged the child. "I'll miss you, darling," he said. "And I love you so much." Chiara opened her mouth to speak, and he kissed her hard. "Love you, too, darling. Thanks for leaving early to take care of the mess at home. See you in two or three sleeps at the most." The boat pulled away, and Tom leaped from the gunnel onto the pier.

"Tom," Chiara shouted, "Watch out...." The noise of the engine swallowed the rest of her words.

Chapter Fifteen

Venice, January 1967

Tom lingered on the pier until the taxi merged into the water traffic on the lagoon. Then he walked toward the gatehouse. Chiara had shouted something that the wind carried off. Probably telling him not to worry, that she'd manage everything till he returned. Normally, he wouldn't doubt she could. But he'd sent them both into an apparent crime scene in their home. God, what wrack and ruin awaited his girls? Chiara would hold up. But little Faith? What would go through her mind when she saw the damage to her room and toys? Thank God, Chiara was strong and intelligent and a smart mother. Still, he knew events had pushed her to the limit. The disappearance of Sona and her family. A cold walking tour of Venice. Mira swooping into their lives. On the pier he'd seen the dark circles under her eyes and heard the hoarseness in her voice when she spoke. It was at least a small comfort knowing they'd all be together again in under thirty-six hours.

Meanwhile he had the conservator to deal with. And quite possibly Mira, too. The woman's story about appraising family treasure seemed like a stretch, though he couldn't say why exactly. And showing up just now at the monastery? Give him a break. He needed to find out more. But time was short since he planned to leave for home in just over twenty-four hours. And he had a full day planned with the conservator, Father Davit. If things went well in the conservatory, he'd have real news to bring Chiara. He picked up his pace.

At their apartment building, he thudded up the stairs that led to the hallway and the Byron Room. He found the abbot and another monk sitting on folding chairs in front of the door. Both men fingered their rosaries, their lips moving in silent prayer. A fat Siamese cat lay curled up in Father Vartan's lap, purring. The cat's head lolled back and forth as the monk stroked its neck. Tom cleared his throat. Father Vartan tucked his rosary into a pocket and scooted the cat onto the floor. With a soft grunt the abbot stood up to introduce Father Davit, the monastery's conservator.

Father Davit, a pudgy, silver haired man, wore a cassock that looked several sizes too small for his build. Tom offered the monk his hand and got a firm grip in return. "The conservatory doesn't see many visitors these days," Father Davit said. "I pray God I can help." He spoke cheerfully and loudly as if a little deaf, and he seemed to Tom to be eager to help. Unlike the other monks he wore no beard.

The abbot coughed gently and said, "Father, in the interest of time I suggest you both leave for the conservatory now. You must excuse me. I meet now with the Countess Borja."

"But of course," Father Davit said. "I will help our

guest in any way I can." Turning to Tom, he said, "We go now to the conservatory. It's located in another building on the grounds. I have prepared all."

The conservatory filled a large, windowless crypt in the basement of a building on the weather side of the island. Father Davit unlocked the outside door and Tom stepped down a narrow staircase and along a passageway lit by dim lights. When they reached the conservatory, Father Davit put his shoulder to a heavy iron door and pushed it open. Rusty hinges creaked. "Humidity," the monk explained. "Watch your head," he said as they ducked under a low lintel and stepped into the room. Tom blinked as his eyes adjusted to the bright light.

Tall, portable heaters spaced out across the floor, glowed red orange in the room, and the gentle wafting of warm air washed around Tom's ears. In one corner he heard the rattling and whooshing of a large machine. He asked the conservator about the noise. "A dehumidifier," Father Davit said as he directed Tom to a set of instruments on the wall. "We keep the temperature between 18 and 21 degrees Celsius and the relative humidity at about 45 per cent. Naturally our closeness to the lagoon and sea are a challenge."

"Makes sense," Tom said, nodding and surveying the room. Down the center ran a row of narrow tables, each with a paper cutter and book press. Scattered up and down the tables were heaps of loose and bound leaves, scraps of vellum, stocks of cardboard. Tom felt something brush up against his leg. He bent over and scratched the head of an ancient dachshund with a belly so low to the ground that the dog swept dust along as he moved about the room.

"That's Leo," Father Davit said. "He welcomes you to my workshop." Tom worked his way over to a wall of tall shelves and read the labels on bottles of solvents, glues, and cleaners. Father Davit took Tom's arm and guided him toward a rack slung with knives, scissors, and blades. "The tools of my trade," he said, nudging Tom toward another worktable. On it lay a wooden cradle holding the *Panarion*, open to the envelope pages.

"So, now we get to work," Father said, rubbing his hands. "Not often I get to do a little surgery on such an old book. Even the abbot takes interest in your little project." The men pulled on cotton gloves and aprons. The conservator opened a drawer under the table and pulled out a leather instrument case. Snapping it open, he swept a hand over a row of *Exacto* blades. He selected the thinnest blade, wiped it with a cloth, and inserted it into the handle. From another case he took a large loupe and handed it to Tom. "Clean the glass with one of the solvents. That one," he said, pointing to a jar with an amber-colored liquid inside. "Then hold the loupe for me while I perform our little surgery."

With Tom holding the magnifier Father Davit rested the blade on the long side of the first envelope page. He pressed the blade against the seam and began to cut. "No, this won't work. Look, we're damaging the velum. "We'll need to use tweezers to pull away the threads." He opened another drawer and found a delicate set. "Steady now with the loupe," he told Tom as he began to pull out the threads.

A slender gap opened in the envelope. Tom held his

breath as he waited for the conservator to pull out the threads from the other sides. "Stop. Wait. What are you doing?" Tom said as the conservator put his blade back into the instrument case. "What about the other stitches?"

"Have a little patience, my young friend," Father Davit said, walking away toward a tall cabinet. He returned a moment later, holding a flat round instrument that looked like a large coin.

"What's that?"

"Camera with a light source and retractable handle," said the monk with a twinkle in his eye. "From my time as an intelligence operative for the Allies." He pulled out the handle, turning the camera into an instrument that looked like a large flat spoon. "I hold the handle and guide the camera between the leaves to take photographs. Then we go to my darkroom."

"May I help?"

"Of course. Hold the envelope just a little open as I insert the camera."

"OK," Tom said, watching the monk move the camera up and down along the inside edge of the vellum. Every few seconds the camera's miniature lamp flashed. Tom counted ten shots. Steady now. This could amount to nothing. Or it could reveal something so grand scholars would die to publish the findings. Not every day a biblical writing lost to history for two millennia shows up.

The conservator talked himself through the procedure, snapping his photographs as he went along. "Only work at the edges of the envelope...Careful now...don't damage the contents." A quarter hour passed before Father Davit removed the camera from between the leaves. Without a word he disappeared into his darkroom. A moment later he called out. "You may help me develop the film, if you wish."

"No thanks. I want to write and code my notes from this morning."

An hour later, Tom found Davit in the darkroom, holding the loupe to the prints drying on a line, his throat so dry he could hardly speak. He whispered to the conservator, "I can make out ruled lines and faded, hand-written Greek letters. All caps. All run together. No word breaks." He turned to Father Davit. "My God. This is unbelievable, wonderful. Just what you'd expect first-century AD Greek to look like." He shook the monk's hand. "Thank you. Thank you. My God. I think it's the autograph—the original letter that Apostle Paul wrote. See the striations up and down the page? Papyrus plant fibers. That's what a first-century AD papyrus leaf looks like."

"Your patience paid off," Father Davit said, "Congratulations."

"Thanks," Tom said, pointing to one of the photos. "That's the first line of the Androgyne Papyrus. I'll translate the Greek for you." Tom bent over the photographs and translated the Greek. "In Christ there is no male or female, no slave or free, no Jew or Gentile...." Tom set the photograph aside, letting a feeling of reverence and awe wash over his body. "That's Apostle Paul speaking to us from across nearly two thousand years," Tom said in a voice so quiet that the conservator had to lean into Tom to hear the words.

With his hand the monk made a sign of the cross over the page. "Blessed be God, forever and ever," he said.

"Father, now we must remove the fragments so we can document what the photos show us."

The conservator's face hardened. He stepped back from Tom. "I'm sorry," he said. "The abbot forbids it. Such an operation will destroy the leaves and the fragments."

Tom grabbed the man by the shoulders. "Wait! You're the conservator. Do your job. You can recover the fragments without destroying the leaves. Scholars, church leaders, the media will never take the Androgyne Papyrus seriously if we only have photos to back up our work."

"I'm sorry," Father Davit said, pushing away from Tom. "The abbot is our final authority in all matters of monastic life, include the library holdings."

The conservator looked at Tom. "Do not lose hope, young man. Today we took a first baby step. Tomorrow or the next day I send the Armenian codex to a colleague at the University of Venice. Infrared photography is her specialty. With her machine she can scan everything inside the three envelopes and send you high-quality photographs.

The hair on the back of Tom's head spiked. "Can you trust her?"

"She is my daughter."

Chapter Sixteen

Venice. January 1967

After Tom, Chiara, and Faith left the refectory Mira sat down with the monks again, lingering over a glass of orange juice, chatting up the men. For a while she made small talk about the weather then asked offhandedly about the American visitors and their reason for staying in the monastery. The monks wagged their heads and turned back to their breakfast. The abbot just smiled and stirred his tea. Well, so much for gathering intelligence from these tight-lipped tablemates. She bid the monks good-bye and excused herself. "Documents to read," she said to the abbot. "See you in a couple of hours to go over the records my family left behind."

"Won't you have a bit of breakfast first?" the abbot asked.

"No thanks. I've ordered the guest master to bring some food to my apartment. Until later."

Crossing the quadrangle, she climbed the stairs to the guest quarters and let herself into her rooms. Yes! There on the marble top bar that separated the sitting and the dining rooms she spotted a bottle of sparkling Spumante poking out of an ice bucket. Next to the ice bucket waited the local snacks she requested: Pickled squid, fried meatballs, sauced vegetables, panini, crostini. She sampled a meatball, then a squid. Delicious. She felt her anxiety melt away. Nothing like Mediterranean finger food to settle a girl's nerves before a mission.

With a panini in one hand, a flute of wine in another she walked to the *en suite*. Pulling off her boots, she undressed and tossed her lingerie, pants, and jacket into a pile on the floor. As the freestanding tub filled, she squirted a long stream of Badedas into the tap water. The gel frothed into a green cloud. Mira caught her breath. Just the minty aroma of horse chestnut and cedar wood already made her feel fresh, clean, and womanly. She patted her butt and tummy. Still flat. She lifted her breasts. Firm enough. She shook her head. Long and luxuriant hair fell to her shoulders. No inner judges to quiet. Not yet anyway.

After a long bath Mira dressed in a businesslike gray suit and accessorized with low heels, gloves, even a sober little hat. Light makeup and a double strand of white South Sea pearls finished her look—steady, aristocratic, stunningly beautiful.

Crossing the compound, she waved at an ancient gardener swinging a heavy scythe at a stand of dead grass and rotting camellia. A wineskin hung around his shoulders, and he held out the tip. "A sip for the old times, or at least against the cold, Contessa?" Mira patted the old fellow's cheek and said, "No thank you," and remembered with fondness the gardeners among whom she'd played as a child on her father's estates in Andalusia. Innocent days so long ago. She tugged on her suit jacket; time to harden up.

It was 8:00 p.m. when Mira finally wrapped up her meeting with the abbot and his insurance agent. She returned to her apartment, trailed by a monk carrying a light supper and bottle of Veneto red on a tray. At the door she sent the man off with a dismissive wave. She was hungry but she owed a report to Abbot Roberto. Sitting down at a marquetry secretary desk, she composed a single page. There was a long and florid thank you for helping her leave Milwaukee before the police could question her in connection with the bombing. She hinted at progress in the matter of Tom Weathering and his project but left things purposefully vague. Time enough later for details. She tucked the letter into a drawer then reached for a bottle of poppy seed juice that Apkar the apothecary left on the secretary. She gulped a mouthful straight down from the bottle to steady her mind, undressed, and threw herself on a sofa to rest for an hour.

At 10:00 p.m. the clock on a side table chimed. Time to dress for work. She belted a lustrous silk kimono over her body, leaving the collar seductively open to a male gaze. The cool glistening fabric always raised goosebumps on her skin, and this evening she expected the wrap to send a carnal shiver down Tom's spine as well. She reached for a pair of three-inch stiletto heels. Always a nice equalizer with a taller man. And in case he had a nose for a woman's scent, she misted her chest and shoulders with the citrusy and powdered leather fragrance of Tabu.

Now her jewel case, Mira took a long hairpin with a diamond-studded hollow end. She snapped open the end cap. Inside lay a massive dose of Kava root sleeping powder. With the pin she set her hair in a casually messy updo, ready at a moment's notice to tumble down her back in a tawny cascade. From the same case she pulled out a gold wrist bangle in the shape of a serpent and slipped it on her wrist. She dropped a small compact case that hid a micro-camera into her kimono's wide pocket. Then, standing up, she went to the liquor cabinet under the bar and studied its contents. She settled on a bottle of Hine cognac.

Locking the apartment behind her, she padded down the corridor to Tom's suite, her stiletto heels dangling from her free hand. No need to clatter past the other rooms and stir up other guests if indeed there were any. A bar of light gleamed under Tom's door. Good. She'd banked on the man working late after his day in the library. To her surprise she heard the pops and ticks of a scratchy phonograph. A frantic aria split the silence inside the room. She placed a hand over her heart. Oh, God! Puccini. La Bohème, no less. She adored the work and its heart-wrenching story of tragic love. She closed her eyes and pressed her fingers to her mouth, picturing Rodolfo, Mimi's lover, taking her lifeless hand and singing, "What a cold little hand." Well, hopefully, Tom would not find her lifeless. Mira put her ear to the door. She smothered a laugh. Tom sang along. And not totally off key. Good God. Her target that evening was a budding baritone. She bent over and slipped into her heels.

She knocked solidly. The music stopped. There was no answer. Shivering in the drafty corridor, she knocked again. Finally, Tom opened the door. "Hi," she said, as Tom, barefoot and holding a toothbrush, filled the door frame. She bit her lip at a near comic scene. There was a dab of toothpaste on his chin. He was missing one sock. His face crinkled in surprise. "Stopped by to ask you to turn the music down."

"Sorry, is it that loud?"

"Loud enough. So, you're an opera aficionado?" she said, dabbing at the toothpaste gob with her sleeve. "There, now you're ready for visitors."

"Hardly. Look. I don't mean to be rude, but I'm on my way to bed. Breakfast tomorrow?" He started to close the door. Mira jammed a foot against the baseplate. "My God, Mira, you're a piece of work. What don't you understand about I'm tired and going to bed? You heard about our home in Göttingen? Not much in the mood for a visitor."

"Well, maybe if we talk awhile, you'll feel better." She gave a wide and generous smile.

"OK. Come in for a minute."

"Thanks. It's freezing out here," Mira said, hunching her shoulders together, offering Tom a glimpse of bare skin. She pushed past him into the apartment. Halfway across the sitting room, she turned and looked at Tom who was still standing in the door frame, hands on hips, head tilted. In his bare feet he was just under six feet. His affable, handsome face and wide shoulders pulled on her like a magnet. Careful now. Don't fall for this charmer.

"You may come in, too," she said brightly, turning her back to Tom and tossing her head so that her hair worked loose from its pin and fell across her neck. She plucked the pin from her hair and dropped it into her pocket. "Aren't your feet cold? Mine are freezing." Tom glanced down. His bare feet poked out of blue and white pajamas sprinkled with images of Gemini spacecraft. "A frustrated astronaut, I see," she quipped.

"Hardly. Gift from Chiara and Faith. We're into silly presents."

Tom ran a hand through his hair, and her mind lingered on the thought of his hands playing with her hair. Stop it, woman. This is business tonight. She looked at her wristwatch. "An hour, no more. Promise."

Chapter Seventeen

Venice, January 1967

"Brought you a gift," Mira said, holding up the bottle of Hine. "Do you drink cognac? We both leave in the morning so we'll make this a good-bye drink." She saw his face brighten at the mention of cognac. Maybe her work this evening would go faster than expected. Tom walked toward her, hitching up his pajamas and reaching for a robe thrown over a chair.

He sniffed the air. "Your fragrance reminds me of Chiara's. What's it called?"

Well, he's perking up a bit. That's good. Go slowly. Be cautious. "Tabu," she said, drawing the collar of her gown suggestively off her shoulder, showing the full curve of a breast. Tom's eyes followed the movement of the gown.

"Why don't you offer a lady a drink?" She gave him a lazy look and held up the bottle of Hine.

Tom said, "I'll open and pour. I've got time for one glass. Then I have some work to finish this evening."

"What? You said you were on your way to bed, you naughty boy."

Mira wagged a finger at him in a playful scold.

"I meant to say I had work to do first."

"Whatever. Look, I think I got crossways with Chiara, maybe with you, too, at breakfast this morning. You're leaving tomorrow, and I'd hate for two Milwaukee Braves fans to quarrel. Just one drink and I promise I'll leave. May I at least use the bathroom and put myself together before you toss me out?"

"Of course. It's through the bedroom to the right."

Mira lingered in the bathroom and by the time she returned, Tom had found two snifters. The bottle of Hine lay open on the glass table in front of the sofa. "Hey, I'm back. Remember me?" She sat down on the couch next to a gilt lamp on an end table, stretching out her legs, kicking off her stilettos. Awkward had passed. Time for charm. She watched him open the bottle and pour cognac expertly into their snifters. He warmed her glass with his hands before offering it to her.

The man had class. Who knew? "Let's drink to you finishing your work and me mine." Mira pointed toward a writing table strewn with sheets of paper. A notebook lay off to the side. "Your report?"

"Yes. No. Notes mostly." Tom started to get up and Mira pulled him down by his robe.

"Leave it. I wouldn't understand anyway."

"Sorry. SOP in research. Always put your work away," he said. "Besides, I hate to leave a mess overnight." At the desk, he tucked his notebook and loose papers into a drawer. "Boring stuff," he said over a shoulder as he slid the notebook to the right side of the drawer. "Research observations. List of things to follow up." He sat down on the sofa again and tipped the lip of his snifter against hers. "Sorry if I'm a little distracted tonight. With Chiara and Faith rushing home to look into the damaged apartment, I've got a lot on my mind."

Mira smiled inwardly. There was no key to the drawer. "Sorry for bad news from home," she said. "And I didn't mean to pry into your work. Just a curious cat." She looked at Tom over the top of her glass, taking his measure. He seemed settled in for a conversation with her, at least for the better part of an hour. "Aren't you cold? I am. "Would you mind bringing a pillow for my back and blanket for my legs? This whole place is so cold and drafty."

"Sure." Tom walked into the bedroom and returned a moment later with a blanket and pillow. He dropped the pillow and blanket on Mira's lap. "I'll let you make yourself comfortable." He sat down at the far end of the sofa.

"Some gentleman you are," Mira said, bracing her back with the pillow and wrapping her legs with the blanket.

"So," Tom asked, "how'd the insurance meeting go today?"

Mira put on a pouty face. Not what she wanted to talk about this evening. She reached for Tom's arm. "Sit closer. I don't want to yell at you." She shifted closer to Tom on the sofa, her hips touching his.

"The meeting?"

"Boring. Too long. Insurance this, insurance that.

Buckets of heirlooms needed a reappraisal. Now your turn." Time for the male ego to preen. She topped off their cognac glasses.

"I'm this close to finding what Chiara and I came for."

"And what's that?"

Tom studied his fingernails then the ceiling.

"Oh come on, Tom. I'm just trying to be social before we...I mean I go to bed. Whoops that didn't come out right. Or did it?"

"Well, OK. Just between us then. Nearly twenty centuries ago a writing that belonged in the Bible went lost. Chiara and I think we know where it is." He held out a thumb and pointer finger and pinched them to within a hair of each other. "We're that close."

"So what if you find the writing? Sell it? Make a fortune?"

"Hardly. I'll hand it over to the university and a publisher. Eventually some progressive leaders in the Vatican will read the work. They might find it helpful."

"Helpful for what?" Mira said. "Rebuilding old churches? Building new Catholic schools?"

"No, more serious than that. It adds force to reforms in the Church that want to protect children against predator clergy and put women in positions of authority and power."

"Whew," Mira said, fanning her face theatrically with a hand. "Not a small thing you want. Well, good for you." She lifted her cognac glass. "Here's to Moses or Jesus or whoever wrote your lost writing." Timing was everything, and she felt a reveal coming.

"Actually, it's a writing from...from a first century AD

Christian author."

"Wow, that's brilliant, Tom. Here's your reward." She brushed her lips against his and moved against him in a body caress. He pulled back. "Wow, do I scare you that much?"

"No," he said with a laugh. "Never kiss on the first date."

"Fair enough." Careful now. Time was slipping by, and she'd not yet scored any real intelligence. "So, tell me about yourself," Mira said, loading her face with a warmth that clashed with the icy calculations running through her mind. She draped an arm over his shoulder. He didn't move away.

For a quarter an hour, Mira listened, first with pretense then with engagement. He was a natural storyteller, plain spoken, funny, thoughtful. Caught up in his small talk, she felt the air in the room thicken and crackle with pleasure. Her pleasure. Damn cognac. An hour ago, she'd come in flint-hard on a mission. Now, she sat like a stupid lump, grinning, nodding, encouraging. She learned about noodling catfish, log rafting, and camping under the stars. She giggled helplessly at Tom's story of a younger sister who glued protruding ears to her head.

When the tower bells rang 11:00 p.m., Mira's own alarm went off. Damn the man. He'd enchanted her for over an hour. Rookie mistake. And possibly fatal if the abbot got wind of her dalliance. Time to get her claws into the man. "My feet have fallen asleep. Be a sport and rub them," she said suddenly, throwing off her blanket and stretching out on the sofa. She dropped her feet on Tom's lap.

"OK. You tell me about yourself," Tom said. "History of the Borja-Borgia family in five minutes."

Mira leaned forward to reach into the opening of her gown. She drew out a cameo locket on a chain and opened the clasp, holding it out to Tom. She caught him looking down her kimono. His face flushed.

"She's beautiful," Tom said. "Who is it? Chiara and Faith love jewelry. I wish they could see it."

"I'll bet they'd love my little bracelet, too," Mira said, holding up her gold bangle and spinning it on her wrist.

"Wow! You can say that again. Looks really old and valuable."

"Phoenician," Mira said. "From some grave goods found in a dig site on our family property in Sicily. I bribed the dig director to give it to me." Mira leaned into Tom, putting the tip of her nose to his. "See what a naughty girl I am?" Her fingers speared through the strands of his hair, dropped to his neck.

"Like I said earlier. I gotta work yet tonight. Enjoyed your company. But that's all that's gonna happen," Tom said, easing himself away. "Chiara and I are too close. I don't fool around with other women. Not even countesses."

Mira gave a laugh that was long and shrill. "In Italy only a homosexual or *castrato* refuses sex with a beautiful woman. You're a real piece of work, Thomas Weathering."

"Before I met Chiara, I'd be all over you. But now I'm, well, a one girl guy. With Chiara I found happiness, a lifetime of happiness if we're lucky. Don't really want to trade that for a toss in the hay with a countess and her

Phoenician jewelry."

"You are a strange man, Tom Weathering."

"Well, Chiara trusted me enough to have our child. Loving those two and keeping them whole has taken over my life." He spun a pearly drop of cognac around the inside of the snifter. "Look," he said, tipping the glass to his lips, "you've been here over an hour. One more glass of this swill and then I'm going to toss you out. Tell me about the lady in the locket…after I use bathroom.

By the time Tom returned to the sofa Mira had refilled their snifters with the last of the Hine and swirled the head of her hairpin around in his glass. She winced at the traces of the Kava root sedative that still hung suspended in the snifter. Tom didn't seem to notice. Still, she kept a watchful eye on the man while she lined up the cardinals, popes, and even a queen of England that filled out her family tree. Finally, at the story of the Borgia's improbable saint—Francis Borgia—his head drooped on her shoulder. She lifted the empty snifter from his hand and stretched him out full length on the sofa, spreading a blanket over him and tucking a pillow under his head. With a kiss on his forehead, she said, "Sleep well, my little rabbit. When you wake up in the morning, I'll be gone. It pleased me to hunt you."

At his writing table, she opened the drawer and found Tom's notebook with a letter folded inside. With her camera she photographed the pages of the notebook. Tom had a good clear hand. Trouble was the pages, in code, didn't make sense, and only Tom had the key. Happily, she had the leverage to get it from him after he returned to

Germany.

She slipped the bangle from her wrist, turning its three twisted cords of gold over in her hand. "My precious one," she said to the bejeweled serpent, "it's now up to you to help me pry secrets from him." In the bedroom she dropped the bangle on the floor, kicking it under the box mattress, out of Tom's sight. In a matter of days, a maid would find the jewelry, and the monastery would mail the bangle back to Tom. If the little trap worked, Chiara would accuse Tom of spending a night with Mira, and then only she, Mira, could make things whole again. For a price.

Chapter Eighteen

When Tom came around the next morning he struggled to sit up on the sofa. The floor buckled under his feet, and he steadied himself on the sofa cushions. His ears rang, and a heaviness had settled in behind his eyes. As the room came into focus, he figured out two things for sure. He and Mira had drunk a whole bottle of cognac. And she had vanished. The bottle lay on the floor. He gave it a kick and sent it spinning across the carpet.

He plodded into the bathroom, tossed down two aspirin, and returned to the living room. He dropped onto the sofa and peered at the two cognac snifters on the table. One still held a good swallow. He tossed it down. A bite from the dog that bit him last night. The other, empty, showed a tan residue on the bottom. Tom swiped a finger across the dregs and touched the sediment to the tip of his tongue. Yuck. The taste of black pepper filled his mouth. Damnation. Kava root. Been a while since he'd gotten high with that sort of thing as a freshman at Gonzaga.

He stood up and let his fingers guide him along a wall to the kitchen. He fumbled with a coffee pot and finally settled it on the stove. A question banged around in his head. Had he done something really stupid the night before? Apart from enjoying Mira's attentions and then letting her dope him?

He cranked his head slowly toward his writing desk. He felt his eyes trying to catch up with his skull. At first he thought the drawer looked closed tight, the way he'd left it. Then he saw an ever so small gap. Oh God. She'd stolen his project notebook. He tried to stand and nearly fell forward on his face. OK, buddy. One step at a time. Pull your pants and shirt on then get your shit together.

At the desk he pulled the drawer open. He let out a long breath. The project notebook with its letter and all his observations still lay inside. The book lay where he'd placed it last night. But upside down. His blood froze. Mira had found his notes. Just curiosity? No. Assume the worst. She probably photographed them if she was any good at her job. The penny fell hard. She'd played him for a fool. Some neighborly, social call last night. Still, she didn't get all she wanted even if she'd photographed the pages. Thanks to Gordon's advice he always wrote his notes in a simple code that would take a good while to unscramble. Well, one thing was a lead pipe cinch. Mira'd be back for a second round of cat and mouse.

It took Tom less than an hour to pack. He made his good-byes to the monks and boarded a *vaporetto* for the Venice train station. On the crossing, he chewed a handful of aspirin he found in his backpack. He nearly threw up when the boat hit choppy water in the middle of the lagoon. To make matters worse, the boatman said it was a pity he'd not boarded the earlier steamboat. He might have shared a ride with a lovely lady also leaving the monastery. What a colossal fool he'd been. Now Mira had a lead—a coded one, but still a lead--on his work at the monastery. Any amateur cryptographer could unravel his code in a matter of minutes. He needed to warn Gordon. But there was no way to get hold of him. Next best thing was to warn FBI agent Shay.

At the train station, Tom found a telegraph office and wired Shay: MIRA BORJA IN VENICE. MORE TO FOLLOW. TOM WEATHERING.

FBI Agent Henri Shay fingered the Western Union telegram he'd received a half-hour earlier from Tom Weathering. News about Mira Borja was a break for the FBI and MPD, with both agencies grasping at straws to find this person of interest. He wanted to return a telegram to Tom, thanking him for the new lead. But he didn't have an address. And the person who did, Dr. Gordon, now lay in a new hospital somewhere out in the county.

So, Mira had high-tailed it to Italy. No wonder she'd eluded MPD's grasp. It was time to alert Customs and Immigration. All of a sudden he felt slow, clumsy, and helpless. Along with Gordon he'd encouraged Tom and his family to escape the Sodality by moving to Germany, and now the Sodality had just paid them a call. A sick fear coiled in his stomach. Dammit it all, he'd sent them into danger, and he owed them a way out. Trouble was the FBI had no authority to protect them overseas.

The bankers chair creaked on its rusted swivel as Shay leaned back from his desk and removed the patch and lid that covered his missing left eye. With an atomizer he sprayed a mist of essential rosemary oil across the muscles and tissues in the hollow socket. No medical reason whatsoever, only devotion to his Chinese grandmother who believed ghosts take up residence in a hollow eye. In a couple of weeks, he'd have his new prosthetic. A better color match than before. And no more subliminal ghost anxiety. He chuckled as he replaced the patch, wondering what the Milwaukee FBI office would think about his family's folk religion.

He sat up, closing a manila folder labeled Vatican Bank. In the file lay case notes on the church bombing, the attack on Dr. Gordon, and the threats on the life of Sona Routanian's family. The file took him back painfully to the day when he'd interviewed Tom and Chiara in the hospital. The memory of a bloodied booty on the hospital bed table still made him bite back a sob. Mercifully the child had survived.

It tied Shay in knots that the MPD—the lead jurisdiction in these cases—didn't connect the bombing, the attack, and the threats on Sona with each other. Even more galling, the MPD showed no interest in the intelligence on Mira Borja and the Sodality the FBI had collected. The intelligence came from a single source--Tom Weathering and Chiara O'Keeffe. MPD brushed it off as campus gossip and rumor. He smelled a conspiracy that looked like it could fall under the provisions of the new 1965 Civil

Rights Act. For a little while longer, he'd grin and bear it. Change lay just around the corner.

Chapter Nineteen

Göttingen, January 1967.

Tom slung his backpack across his shoulders and worked his way through a rush hour crowd in the Göttingen station and then headed toward the tram stop on the *Bahnhofsallee*. There he boarded Number 21, claiming an empty seat and lowering a window to let a spray of cool night air blow into his face. From Venice he'd sent Henry Shay a telegram, alerting him to Mira's arrival in Venice.

As Number 21 clanked slowly up a hill toward the *Nonnensteig* stop, the tension that wracked Tom since leaving Venice reached a flashpoint. "Can't you make this damned trolley go faster?" he shouted at the driver. Everyone but the driver turned and stared. "Sorry," he said. "Bad hair day."

The outburst helped. The damaged apartment could be fixed. But what about a weary Chiara and a terrified Faith? He worried especially about Chiara. How to tell her about the hash of things he'd made with Mira the night before. Inviting that woman into the apartment was an unforced error. What a jerk he was. Mira played him like a trout on a hook. The whole thing made him feel cheaper and dumber than a backyard tattoo. Long ago he and Chiara had promised never to hold secrets, even hurtful ones. She'd always kept her side of the bargain. Now it was his turn.

The tram bell clanged to announce his stop. Tom grabbed his backpack and with a wave at the motorman stepped off. Under the soft glow of an overhead streetlamp, he passed in front of Mutti's house. A curtained light showed in a front window. Surely Chiara and Faith had moved in with Mutti for a day or so. Circling around the block, he cut through an ally that led to the back door of their apartment. When he pulled up a few feet from the door he saw a broken pane of glass and bands of yellow tape crisscrossing the door. He swept away the tape and reached for the door handle, cutting the back of his hand on a jagged edge. He stepped into the sunroom.

CRIME SCENE screamed strands of yellow tape crisscrossing doors from the sunroom to the kitchen and two bedrooms. Two faltering steps into the darkness brought him inside the room. He stumbled over solid objects spilled across the tile floor. Wooden blocks and puzzle pieces. "Chiara, Faith," he called, his voice rasping. "Are you here?" No of course not. They had to be at Mutti's. This was a crime scene. The destruction made him gasp for breath. In the darkness he listened and watched like a wild animal scenting danger. Now a full-blown, cold panic froze his blood. What if they'd been home when the rampage broke out?

He ran a hand over a wall until he found the light switch and lit up the room. Their home lay in shambles.

Chairs and tables upended. Lamps shattered. Photos and prints askew on the walls. Curtains flung from their rods. He called their names again, knowing they would not answer. There was only silence and dread. He jumped over bookshelves and cabinets that lay toppled on the floor. Glass shards from a broken window crunched under his feet. He looked at his hand. He bled from a cut in his palm.

Stepping into their bedroom, he stopped short as he saw the smashed remains of his portable Olympic on the floor. Across a mattress borrowed from Mutti ran a jagged gash that looked like a crooked smile. The eiderdown from Mutti's comforter formed a white swath of confetti across the floor.

Rage and remorse clogged his thinking. Tears drizzled down his cheeks. Who did this? The question was rhetorical. He knew the answer. The Sodality. Of that he was sure. What kind of monsters peopled that secret society? No wait. Maybe he was the monster for dragging Chiara and Faith into this world.

He ran into Faith's room. A gutted mattress and a slash pile of ruined dolls and plush toys heaped against one wall. Only a shelf of wood blocks, crayons, finger paints, and story books remained of Faith's work center.

At first, he didn't hear the calling of his name from outside. Then he did. It was Mutti's voice fluting across the fenced yard and through the open back door.

"Tom, Tom, are you home? Is that you? I saw a light. It's Mutti."

He jumped up and plowed through the sunroom to the backdoor. From the fence line between their apartment and

Mutti's house, a powerful beam blinded him. He flung a hand over his eyes.

"Tom, over here," Mutti said. "Hurry, I'm freezing." She directed her flashlight at the fence gate. "Your family's safe in my house," she said in a steady voice.

"Our apartment is trashed. Are Chiara and Faith safe?"

"Yes, yes. Now come with me and get warm."

Tom opened the gate and hugged Mutti long and hard nearly crushing the slight figure in a shawl and knit cap. He walked alongside Mutti as she flashed a light on the path to her back door. Inside, he saw Chiara sitting at the dining room table next to Faith, who sat in a highchair. He bounded across the floor in two steps. "Oh my God, I'm so glad to see you two," he cried, taking Chiara's hands in his own. "I so feared for your safety!" He reached for Faith and hugged the child until she said, "Blood, Papa."

Chiara sprang from her chair and wrapped Tom's hand in a paper napkin. "I'll find some antiseptic and bandages," she said. "Oh Tom, Tom, I'm so glad you're home. Faith and I missed you so much." She pressed a warm, damp cheek to Tom's face.

"Are you two really OK?" Tom asked, holding Chiara at arm's length. "I feared the worst when I saw our apartment."

"Of course. We're just fine," Chiara said, sitting down again. "Mutti got the telegram I sent from Venice. Phil picked us up at the Göttingen train station and brought us straightaway here.

"So, do you know who broke in? Do the police?" Tom asked.

"No," Chiara said. "Still under investigation. Police were here for three hours today. Let's talk tomorrow, please. Faith and I just want to snuggle you."

"I put your girls up in the garret," Mutti said, "because Phil and Anna are still here. Anna prepares some dinner for you."

"Thanks," Tom said, "I am hungry." He wiped a cheek smudgy with tears and dust. His voice quavered.

Tom reached for a glass of water that Mutti poured. He drank it off. It was good to be in this house, in a safe, orderly home, with the Sodality locked out. For the moment at least. He laid an arm around Chiara's shoulder, kissing her cheek. He touched Faith's forehead. It was cool. "Fever's gone."

"Yes," Chiara said. "Yarrow tea," she said. "Who knew?"

For the first time in two days, Tom felt whole again. The girls were his life, the guardians of everything good about him and the world and the Project. As a couple, he and Chiara were blissfully happy and fully alive. As parents they overflowed with that happiness, felt even more alive. Now, the Project threatened to tear all this apart.

Tom looked into Chiara's face. There was a new set to her jaw, a flare to her nostrils. Her gray-green eyes glinted with some flinty emotion he hadn't seen before. Had she reached the limit of her patience? Did she want to go home? He knew he might well want to. Still, it would be more like Chiara to say something like, "Don't worry, we're safe. Let's get on with it."

With a rattle of plates and cups, Anna strode into the

room, pushing a serving cart heaped with a cozy-wrapped pot of tea and platters loaded with cheese wedges and rough-cut bread slices. Phil carried a porcelain bowl of quark mixed with onions and chives.

"Welcome home, Tom," Phil said, putting the bowl in the center of the table. "Hope you like Mutti's version of fresh-set cheese. Guess you know about the spot of bother while you were away practicing monastic virtues."

Tom smiled at Phil's attempt at humor. "You could say that." He steadied his cup while Anna poured tea. "I thought you two would be back in Oxford by now."

"Needed to top off a few items," Anna said. "We're packed and ready to leave as soon as Phil polishes an essay for his Medieval English tutor."

Tom picked at his late supper then pushed away from the table. Chiara stifled a yawn with a fist. "Girls," he said, "Time for bed." He turned to Mutti, Phil, and Anna. "Thanks for the telegram you sent to Venice and now for taking in Chiara and Faith."

Mutti said. "That's what neighbors do." She turned to leave the room. "Oh, Tom, I nearly forgot. Professor Zimmer called this morning. Please be at his office tomorrow at 10 a.m. He's holding some mail for you."

"News from home. Wonderful. Thanks."

In the garret, Tom changed Faith into her onesie and put her to sleep with a story. Then he and Chiara undressed and pulled the feather comforters up to their chins. They lay entwined in each other's arms, talking in undertones. Through the garret window sparkled starlight and moonlight and the promise of even more cold. Then Tom felt Chiara, warm and pliant, roll on top of him, kiss him hard on the mouth. Yes, yes, and yes. And then there were only shuddering sighs.

Afterwards, they lay side by side again. "Tell me about Father Davit, the conservator," Chiara said.

Tom went over the monk's delicate surgery, the cutting of the threads on the first envelope page, and the sliding of a micro-camera between the two leaves.

"And then?" Chiara asked, propping herself up on an elbow.

"And then," Tom said, "fragments of a writing showed up on the photographs that Father Davit developed."

"Tom, that's wonderful, congratulations," Chiara said. "What's next?"

"Davit sent the *Panarion* to Venice University for an infrared scan of the envelope pages. A specialist will make photographs of the scans and send them directly to Zimmer."

"I'm so happy for you, Tom. For us."

"Thanks, darling. I'll rest easier when we have the photographs in hand."

Chiara settled back in her pillow. "May I ask you something that's been on my mind?"

"Of course."

"Did you see Mira after I left?"

Chapter Twenty

Göttingen, January 1967

"Yeah," Tom began, picking his words carefully. "I did see her after dinner…the day you left. She came up to our apartment around ten that night. "We had a drink, well, two actually, and talked about her family and mine."

Tom snuggled closer to Chiara. She pulled away. For a while he said nothing. A knot twisted his belly. How to talk to Chiara about an evening where Mira came on to him and he managed to endanger the Project? True, it was hardly a whole evening. Only a little more than an hour. But she'd charmed and disarmed him before knocking him out with a drug.

He put a hand on her shoulder. She moved farther away. He dreaded this moment. A lie or a half-truth felt cowardly. He owed Chiara an honest account, if only he himself knew the truth of the evening. He promised himself he'd set things right with the woman he loved more than life itself.

"Look," Chiara said wearily. "Stay on your side of the bed. I know there's a longer story, maybe even a plausible one. But I'm so bone tired and need to get some sleep. Talk tomorrow. Good night." She rolled away to the far side of the bed.

In the morning, Tom dressed Faith and carried her to the kitchen. He warmed her milk then drank a coffee with Phil, Mutti, and Anna. When Chiara joined them thirty minutes later, she settled between Mutti and Anna and listened to the two women roll out a plan to clean up the apartment. Chiara looked up to say, "Tom, don't forget your 10 a.m. meeting with Zimmer. He's also holding some mail for you."

"On my way," Tom said, excusing himself and grabbing his coat on the hallway rack. They did not talk about Mira that day or the next.

When Tom stepped into Zimmer's outer office, Lisle, his graduate assistant, held up a hand. "Better tiptoe in. The old fellow's fit to be tied this morning. He told me that Mutti, I mean Frau Wilhelm, called him last night. Told him burglars wrecked your apartment. He's totally bummed."

"Thanks," Tom said, wondering if Chiara had told Mutti about his foolishness with Mira Borja. If so, what were the chances that Mutti had also passed that on to Zimmer as well. He'd find out soon enough. He knocked on Zimmer's door and walked in without waiting for an invitation. "Good morning, sir."

Zimmer stood at a window, looking down on the square below, his head pressed against the glass. His right hand worked a muscle on the back of his neck. A silver-handled walking stick—one Tom hadn't seen before—

leaned against a radiator under the window. He saw two letters with American stamps on Zimmer's desk.

"So, you have arrived," Zimmer said, still staring out the window. "Welcome home. You must be worn flat from the trip and dealing with the break-in." He reached for his cane and slowly pivoted to face Tom. Zimmer pointed Tom to a chair and settled himself at his desk. How are Chiara and Faith?"

"Coping. Thank God for Mutti."

"And you?"

"In shock. But no more so than Chiara and Faith. Apartment's a total wreck."

"Yes, I know," Zimmer said. "Frau Wilhelm told me you and Chiara met an old friend from Milwaukee in Venice. An Italian named Mira Borja."

Sheesh. That cat got out of the bag damned fast. "We did see Mira."

"An odd coincidence, don't you think? Personally, I might have wondered if the lady didn't have some mischief on her mind. Just saying."

"Mischief? Yeah, I guess you could call it that. She drugged me."

"Hmm," Zimmer said. "Drugged you, did she? Really now? Feel like talking about it?"

"Well, she's a charmer, sir. Came up to the apartment late at night with a bottle of decent cognac and indecent intentions. Slipped a sedative in my drink and..."

Zimmer held up both hands. "Spare me the details, Tom. Just tell me this. Did she get her hands on your project notes?"

"She likely photographed my research notes. Mostly technical measurements and observations on the condition of the envelope pages and their contents."

"Tell me you coded those findings."

"Yeah, I did, thank God. Mira won't make much sense of my gobbledygook. I used a version of Morse code."

Tom gave Zimmer a closer look. His mentor seemed older, almost ghostly. Worry pooled in his eyes. There was a sallow cast to his skin, and folds hung on his facial bones like crepe paper.

"You doing OK, professor?" Tom asked, genuinely worried about the man.

"Yes and No. We'll talk about what's on my mind in a bit. First, tell me what you discovered when you worked on the *Panarion*.

Tom pulled his notebook out of a backpack and placed it on the desk. For a half an hour he decoded his project notes for Zimmer. Going back to the discovery sent a new tingle down his spine. He wrapped up by telling Zimmer that the conservator had sent the *Panarion* to a university college in Venice.

"Why?" Zimmer asked. "That was risky."

"For infrared photographs of the fragments inside, rock-solid proof that the Androgyne Papyrus actually exists."

"You should be pleased with yourself," Zimmer said. "At least I hope so. Now about you and Chiara. How are you both doing after all that's happened in the last days?"

"To tell the truth, Chiara and I feel like there are targets on our backs. Seems all we think about is the break-in and the return of Mira into our lives."

Zimmer said, "I fear for your safety, too. In a moment we must talk about that." He handed Tom the letters. "Sorry, nearly forget these were here. Take a moment to read. I need to stand up."

One letter came from Joseph Terwilliger, their friend and the former owner of the Spudnut Shop in Milwaukee. The handwriting, barely readable, sprawled across the page in a curly, round script. Joseph apologized for not writing sooner and said he sometimes regretted selling the Shop. But now, after settling things with the IRS and the mob in Milwaukee, he planned to travel to Europe, maybe visit them in Göttingen. He'd earned some spending money helping FBI agent Henri Shay. In fact, he and the agent got on so well they might even travel together.

The other letter, though it was a stretch to call it a letter, came from Tom's childhood friend, Mike Mathis. There was just a single line in caps. TEMPORARY DUTY ASSIGNMENT HEIDELBERG. Well, that came as a surprise. A welcome one.

"Tom," Zimmer broke in, "if you're done reading, I want to make a phone call that concerns you and Chiara. Please listen. I'm hoping to reach Professor Dabelstein in Heidelberg."

"Sure thing," Tom said, "I recall Dabelstein and you were POWs together in Russia. Along with Professor Wilhelm. That's where you three learned about the existence of the Androgyne Papyrus."

"That's right." Zimmer reached out and straightened the gulag photograph on his desk.

Suddenly, Tom felt wary. Shouldn't he first know what the call was about? He said, "If you and Professor Dabelstein plan to talk about our future, then please tell me what's going on before you ring him up."

"Of course. My apologies. I am too hasty. Actually, I spoke with Dabelstein already yesterday. We both agreed you cannot stay in Göttingen."

"What the hell? Why not?" The startling news got his blood up. He rose out of his seat and leaned into Zimmer. "I know we're running risks even with you watching our backs. Still, I can handle myself. Chiara, too. We put up a pretty good fight back in Milwaukee."

"This is not Milwaukee, your home turf. This is Europe, the Sodality's territory. Its operatives have traced you to Göttingen…" He didn't finish the sentence. "What I'm saying is that Heidelberg is safer. Dabelstein has resources that I don't have. He's our best, maybe our only hope to secure a home for you and continue the Project." Zimmer reached for the phone on his desk. As he dialed, he said, "If you agree, he is willing to take you on as his assistant."

Tom seized Zimmer's hand. "Wait. What if Chiara and I don't leave?" He heard the line ring on the other end and shot Zimmer a quick question. "What if we stay in Göttingen? I'm not sure we're up to another move so soon. We have Faith to think about."

"You must go. My health is not good. I'll retire soon."

"But…"

"Hello, Erich, this is Zimmer. How are you? How's Erika? Good. Glad to hear it. Look, I'm calling to confirm our plans for Tom Weathering and his family."

Ten minutes later, Zimmer hung up. "So, it is settled."

"Whoa! Wait. Not so fast." There was heat in Tom's face. He clenched a fist and pounded the desktop. "Dammit to hell. I need to talk with Chiara about the whole thing."

Zimmer blinked a look of surprise. "Chiara? Oh...oh ...yes, of course."

Tom looked at Zimmer. "She already knows, right?"

Zimmer arched his eyebrows and held out his hand helplessly. "Frau Wilhelm—Mutti—and I talked with her yesterday. The women agree on the move." A smile curled around the corners of his mouth. "My wife decides such matters, too."

"Well, not in our family, I'm afraid," Tom said, growing angrier at the turn of events. "God dammit, I'm not one to cut and run at the first whiff of gun powder. And I don't think Chiara is either. With all due respect, sir..."

"Tom," Zimmer said, "You're not listening. I can't protect you, Chiara, and Faith after I retire. If you're not worried about yourself and Chiara, then at least consider the safety of your child. She's as much at risk as you are."

Tom stood up, confused and angry. He paced back and forth in front of a bookcase until he got control of himself. Of course, Zimmer was right. The Sodality didn't care a whit about Faith and Chiara, would threaten and kill them if it meant getting to the Papyrus. And probably Mutti, as well. He turned to look at Zimmer. "OK, you win. Heidelberg it is. I guess we should go over the photographs of the fragments we found in the envelope pages.

"Later. Put all that in your report. I suggest you go

home, help with the clean-up of the apartment. And get some rest."

On the tram ride home, Tom warmed up to the prospect of moving to Heidelberg. For one thing, Chiara had job prospects there. For another, the US Army had stationed his friend Mike Mathis at one of the local bases. He made a mental note to himself. Send Mathis a telegram with their childhood signal to stand by for action: Rattlesnake Mountain. And call FBI Agent Henry Shay. He owed the man updates on Mira Borja, the Project, and the upcoming move to Heidelberg.

Chapter Twenty-One

Milwaukee, January 1967

FBI Agent Henry Shay jotted down notes as Tom Weathering told him about Mira Borja, the apartment, and an upcoming move to Heidelberg. After asking Tom to stay in touch, he hung up and pushed away from his desk. His gut told him it would not be the last time he heard from the young American. He swung around in his chair, stood up, and straightened the photos, mementoes, and service awards that ran up and down the wall. He lingered for a few minutes reliving his service to his country. Funny how easy it was to remember the wins and forget the losses. He hoped Tom and Chiara learned this survival skill.

Two autographed black and white photographs took pride of place in the collection. One bore the signature of President Lyndon B. Johnson, the other the signature of FBI Director J. Edgar Hoover. Next to them, in a faded colored print, French President Charles de Gaulle dubbed him a Knight of the Legion of Honor, France's highest military award. An inscription across the foot of the photograph read: *En mémoire de la bataille de Dien Bien*

Robert Hodgson, Jr.

Phu 13 Mars-7 Mai, 1954.

Shay cherished that photo. It took him back a lifetime and several identities ago. As a twenty-one-year-old American volunteer for the French Expeditionary Force in Vietnam, he'd piloted a vintage B-17 bomber.

Now, what was he today? Well, for one thing, a senior FBI agent. For another a Chinese-French-Canadian-American mutt. Around the office, he joked about his mixed heritage, partly to gauge colleagues' response to someone who looked so different.

He reached for a bamboo frame and aligned it with the other photos. Inside the 3'x3' square stretched a large fragment of a ragged and coarsely woven carpet. A gift from his maternal Chinese grandmother. Barely visible in the warp and weft swam three dragons in faded colors of red, white, and blue across a wavy sea.

"It's all that remains of your Chinese family," his grandmother told him years earlier upon presenting him with the carpet fragment. "Everything else, everyone else disappear in the Revolution of 1911."

Two lights on Henri Shay's desk phone blinked at the same time. Shay punched the one for his secretary. "Yes, Viola?"

"It's MPD on the line."

"What do the boys in blue want?"

"You at a crime scene. I'll get the location. And I'll take a message from the other party. It's probably your bookie."

"Very funny," Shay said, picking up a memo he'd just written for Viola. Pulling on his trench coat, gloves, and porkpie hat, he strode out of his office and handed Viola the message. "Call Inspector Dubois at Interpol. Read him the contents of this note. It's got information on the whereabouts of Mira Borja."

Viola looked up at Shay over her glasses. "So you got the skinny on our larcenous countess?"

"Yeah, thanks to a call from a source in Venice."

"Don't forget your galoshes," Viola said to the door as it closed behind Shay.

When Shay arrived at the crime scene, he stomped across slushy snow to the West Canal Street Bridge that spanned the Menomenee River. Damn, he wished he'd thought to pull on his galoshes. Peering into the slushy ice that choked the waterway around the Bridge, he guessed a body had bobbed to the surface when the ice layer melted.

"Hey, Shay, over here."

Turning around, Shay spotted two MPD detectives, Aaronson and Weston. Last October he'd met them in Milwaukee General Hospital after the church bombing. The two detectives stood inside a perimeter of yellow tape, hands jammed into their field coats. Aviator style hats, flaps up, covered their heads. "Come join us," Aaronson shouted above the screech of an approaching ambulance and fire truck.

"So, what have you got here?" Shay asked. "Besides wet feet?"

Weston jabbed a finger at Shay's muddy loafers. "And you're ribbing us about duck feet?"

Aaronson said, "The river and the whole goddamned

city are one squishy carpet of ice 'n snow," He jabbed a finger in the direction of a squad car parked on the bridge. "Got two young kids in the car."

Weston jumped in, "The kids skipped school. Wanted to play some shinny hockey on the river but didn't like the look of the ice. Instead, they found a bridge jumper. Guess the thaw floated the dead guy up from under the river ice."

"What's the incident have to do with the FBI?" Shay asked.

"A little respect, please. Might be a person of interest for you feds," Weston said, jabbing a finger at one of the bridge pylons. "Boys found him about there, all goggle-eyed and bloated." He gave a coarse laugh. "Scared the pee out of the little buggars. Serves 'em right for skipping school."

Shay said, "I'll talk to them in a bit. I appreciate you calling me in. Still not sure why. He knew the two detectives enjoyed stringing him along. He'd wait them out. "I'm sure the boys are terrified. Called the parents?"

"Yeah," Weston said, "then we called you. Our LT figured you might be interested."

"Give him my thanks," Shay said, still not sure why the MPD had called in the FBI. He'd find out soon enough. Two white-suited assistants from the coroner's office lifted a body into an open black bag and zippered the corpse inside. Shay sucked in a long breath as the zipper tab purred along the teeth like a tiny engine and covered the face of the vic. He'd already loaded enough body bags into his B-17 for a lifetime.

The white-suits pushed the gurney under a yellow tape,

pulling up at the coroner's van. A figure dressed in a wet suit stepped from behind the open rear door. Shay recognized LeRoi Lavesque. "Hey, LeRoi," Shay said, "Been awhile."

"Show has," said LeRoi, a Cajun transplant with a sorghum-thick accent.

"What's the prelim?" Shay asked.

"Cain't say," the diver said with a shrug of his shoulder. "Tank God he had some ID. River's full wit pike and catfish. Near et 'im up. Ever' thing 'cept his wristwatch, and that sucker's still tickin'."

"Name of the vic?"

The two detectives came up behind Shay. "J. Barriston Gordon," Aronson said. "Driver's license and Marquette faculty card IDed the body. You remember the guy from the church bombing, don't ya?"

Shay's gut caved in. God. Was this another casualty of the militia crazies and the damned race for some lost Bible book? He hadn't seen Gordon since the hospital interviews following the church bombing and the attack on Gordon in the chapel. A decent fellow. A little wooly headed. Still the professor hovered over Tom and Chiara like a Dutch uncle. "That was Tom Weathering's advisor," Shay said. "I interviewed him twice. Once after the church bombing and then again after someone attacked him in the university chapel."

"Yeah, I recall the couple. They liked to play detective and look what it got 'em?" Aaronson said, stripping off his field jacket and tucking his cap under an arm. "Whew. I'm sweatin' in these rags. So, where's those folks now?"

"Not sure," Shay said. He'd play his cards close to his chest and keep Tom's location and phone call to himself. "Do you think I could look at the police report and the ME's paperwork when you have it? Like to add a copy to my files."

Weston said, "Gordon's a MPD case. Nothing to do with the feds."

Shay returned his most disarming smile. "Of course, it's a MPD case, and I'm glad for the courtesy of an invitation to the scene. Still, Gordon's a person of interest to the FBI." He offered Weston a lozenge from a tin in his pocket. "As Tom's advisor, he may know—well, knew—something about the church bombing and the disappearance of Sona Routanian. And there's this—he had hate mail from some upcountry militia group."

"We gotta get permission from our LT," Aaronson said.

"Sure. You do that, ask the lieutenant." No need to ruin their day and tell them the FBI had already folded up everything into one federal case. "Oh, just one more thing."

"Jesus, now what?" Weston grumbled out of the side of his mouth to Aaronson.

"Be glad for any new leads your lieutenant has on these names. He pulled out a pad and pen from his trench coat pocket. He wrote down: Mira Borja (former Marquette grad student), Carlito (Sicilian bartender at Mader's), Edward Campbell (Marquette theology prof). Shay tore off the sheet and handed it to Weston.

"What's this got to do with our latest vic?" Weston asked after reading the names out loud.

"Maybe nothing. Just a hunch. Be glad for some background."

"Hunch? Give us something more for the LT."

Shay lifted a shoe from the slush. His feet were soaked, and dabs of mud spattered his pant cuffs. He'd die right now for a hot cup of tea. "Big picture only. FBI's looking into a conspiracy to violate civil rights. Based on the '64 Civil Rights Act.

"Violate civil rights?" Aaron snorted back.

"Based on your freedom to practice religion," Shay said. It was as good a case as he could make on the spot. He prayed he'd have something more solid soon.

"1964 Civil Rights Act?" Aaronson said, laughing and rolling his eyes. "Weston, you ever heard of such a thing?"

"Hell, yes," Weston said. "Our LT gags every time a bleeding-heart Perry Mason brings it up in court. Pain in the ass for cops. Gives us fits trying to keep track of commies, Panthers, and all the other kooks in the city."

"Back to the vic," Shay said. "Gordon didn't strike me as a suicide or drunk." Shay gave the back of his head a scratch. "When I interviewed the vic, he was stable, full of life, just the right amount of eccentric. He really cared for Tom and his—." Shay saw the detectives had tuned him out. "Please bring the reports when we meet next week Monday."

"Next week Monday?" Aaronson said, jerking his head up in surprise. "Since when do you call the shots for us?"

Shay shuffled his feet and kicked at a chuck of ice. He looked straight at Aaronson. "Since I asked your LT to send you over. There's someone I want you to meet on background in my office. 9 a.m. sharp." Shay turned and walked to his car. As he drove off, he glanced into his rearview mirror and smiled at the detectives' Bronx cheer.

Chapter Twenty-Two

Milwaukee, January 1967

Agent Shay stood at his fifth-floor office window, looking down at the brisk Monday morning foot traffic on East Kilbourne Avenue. "Right on time," Shay said to FBI Agent René Crockett who stood next to him. "There's Weston and Aaronson. They just double parked their squad car and headed for the entrance. They'll be here in ten minutes. Any questions before they arrive?"

"Nope. I'm good. Wanna call down to Security and have their old beater hauled off?" Crockett asked with a wink. She was a tall, striking woman with an infectious sense of humor, and one of the few black females in the Milwaukee office.

Shay laughed and shook his head. He rarely met visitors in his office, more often booking one of the large conference rooms. But today he wanted a smaller setting for his meeting, and his office suited him just fine.

In the hallway outside his office, the tramping of hard-soled shoes announced Weston and Aaronson. Agent Crockett saw the men in and introduced herself.

Clutched in Aaronson's hand were two brown folders. From the labels Shay recognized an MPD crime scene report and a file from the Milwaukee County Medical Examiner. Yes. This was promising. Shay nodded at the two plain clothes detectives. They'd swapped out their usual slouchy, wrinkled slacks and jackets for freshly pressed suits and polished shoes. The smell of Old Spice— a bit too generously applied for Shay's taste—wafted from closely shaven faces.

As Shay seated the detectives and took their coats, another man, smelling of campfire smoke, stepped into the office. Tall and heavily bearded, his bulging muscles strained against a tight-fitting tactical parka. With his woodsman's boots and boogie hat, the man looked out of place in a suit-and-tie FBI office.

After giving the newcomer a warm greeting and generous handshake, Shay took his coat. "This is Mick Wallingford," Shay said to the MPD detectives, who eyed the scruffy man before offering a handshake and a halfhearted, "Pleased to Meetcha."

Wallingford returned a wide grin. "Didn't have time to freshen up. Just in from an undercover field assignment. I've got to return to my lair in an hour." He spoke with a refined Harvard accent that commanded instant authority.

Shay offered Wallingford a chair, explaining to the MPD detectives that the agent worked undercover for Alcohol, Tobacco, Firearms, and Explosives. "I've asked him to brief us on the militants in the Dells that we're tracking. Mind if I take a gander at the two reports first?"Shay held out his hand for the files. "I'll just flip through a few pages," Shay said. "Talk amongst yourselves."

When he looked up a few minutes later, he let loose a sigh that was half frustration, half disbelief. The ME and the MPD accounts didn't match. The latter gave the cause of death as suicide or accidental drowning. The former treated the case as a possible homicide, the result of blunt force trauma to the head.

Shay glared at the two detectives, who seemed eager to study their shoes laces. "These two reports don't match," Shay said. "MPD says suicide, the ME blunt force trauma."

"Yeah, we saw that," Weston said. "Our LT says we gotta go with our report. He's got witness statements that say the guy had the DTs and depression. Hadn't shown his face on campus for a couple of weeks."

Shay fought back a temptation to tongue lash the two detectives. But now was neither the time nor place to get sideways with the MPD. He had a civil rights case to build, and he'd need all the local help he could muster. Instead, he tented his hands, worked up his most inscrutable face and hoped for a Zen moment of restraint. "Need a copy for the office," he said, pulling a roll of *Lifesavers* from a drawer and popping a green ring into his mouth. He crunched the sweet slowly.

"Mind if we smoke?" Weston asked.

"Go ahead." Shay put the *Lifesavers* back in the drawer. He couldn't resist pulling the detectives' chain a little bit. "So, here's a question." He waited until the two men lit their cigarettes and took a deep draw. "In your experience how many drunks and jumpers beat themselves around the head before they fall or jump?" He held up one of the photos from the ME's report.

"Never heard of such a thing," Aaronson said, flicking ash in his pant cuff.

"In this photo the back of Gordon's head looks like mashed potatoes."

"Ah, that," Weston said with relief. "Force of the fall from the bridge."

"Not unless he did a back dive," Shay said. "I'd guess blunt instrument trauma. Our lab at Quantico can tell the difference. I'm sending a copy of the report to them. We might want our coroner to redo the autopsy."

"What the hell? No way. We got good forensics on the vic."

Shay popped another *Lifesaver* into his mouth. "Detectives, a lot has changed in the last three days. Agent Crockett, will you and Agent Wallingford start things off?"

"Sure thing," Crockett said. "Agent Wallingford works undercover for the ATF and we seconded him about a year ago on the case. Hell, Wally, why don't you tell your own story?"

"Delighted to do so. Two years ago last December I went undercover. Infiltrated a militant compound in the Dells. We had evidence of weapons trafficking and racketeering." Crockett reached over and flicked a tick off Wallingford's sleeve. "Thanks. Anyway, ATF contacted Agent Shay here when we learned that the good old boys in the Dells do contract killings, robbery, and kidnapping—anything for the right price."

"Good Catholic boys with criminal minds? Who'da

thunk it," Weston said, taking a poke at his partner's ribs with an elbow. "Beat's a Friday night Catholic fish fry."

Crockett said, "Wally tied the group to a failed bank robbery and suspected murder at the Marine National Exchange Bank. Contract work for a shady operation in the Vatican Bank known as the Sodality.

"Yeah, we worked both cases, too," Weston said. "And the church bombing and the disappearance of Sona Routanian."

"I know," Agent Wallingford said. "That's why we're all here. A little coordination."

Shay stood up. Time to spring his surprise. "The FBI now leads this investigation, which we plan to prosecute under Civil Rights and RICO statutes. What until now has looked like isolated crimes, turns out, we think, to be part of a larger conspiracy." Shay ticked the pieces off on his fingers. "Bank robbery, church bombing, death of Professor Gordon, disappearance of Sona Routanian, flight of Mira Borja. Though out of our jurisdiction, I could also add the murder of Professor Wilhelm in Göttingen as well as the recent home invasion that terrorized Tom Weathering and his family in the same German city."

Reaching over his desktop, he picked up a copy of a fat manila folder. From inside he pulled Xerox copies of two letters. "This one," he said to the detectives, handing them a sheet, "is a request from MPD to the FBI, asking us to take over jurisdiction in these cases. And this one is a copy of a letter signed by the FBI Special Agent in charge of the Milwaukee office, accepting jurisdiction." Shay looked the detectives straight in the face.

Weston gave a whinny of distress and ran a hand over the top of his head. A small vein over one of Aaronson's eyebrows bulged. Shay had seen cops go ballistic for less. With a loud snort Weston reached inside his coat. Agent Crockett took a step forward, her own hand plunging inside her jacket, before pulling it back. Weston produced his own sheets of paper. "Got our copies this morning. Sorry if we gave you a hard time. Nuttin' personal. MPD's kinda protective of its turf. Right Aaronson?" The other detective nodded. "Our LT says you got our full cooperation."

"Thanks for that, detectives. Now here's some intelligence the FBI can share with you." Opening a file cabinet, he pulled out a sheaf of case notes. "Field Report on Mira Borja, the exchange student who skipped town. She turned up in Venice, among other places."

"Jesus," Aaronson said, as Shay dropped the report back in the cabinet. "She musta had a diplomatic passport to slip out of the country like that. You got a copy of her paperwork for us? You gotta know the lady's a person of interest at MPD, too."

"Interpol puts her on the payroll of the Sodality," Crockett said. "Specializes in assassinations, gathering intelligence; you know, a real Betty Crocker homebody."

"Sodality?" Aaronson asked, crinkling his forehead.

"Rogue operation inside the Vatican Bank," Shay explained. "Outsources its wet work to nice folks like the militiamen and shooters like the Borja gal."

"Wet work? Vatican Bank?" Both detectives looked thunderstruck. "Who'd thunk it," Weston said. "Been Catholic all my life. Never heard of dat Sodality."

Wallingford said, "Targets anything and everything that threatens the old ways in the Catholic Church, like male privilege. Goes after radical priests and nuns, racially mixed congregations, civil rights advocates, anti-war protesters."

Agent Crockett said, "I'm guessing there's a simple and elegant answer to the question of who's behind the bank robbery, assaults, hate mail, murders, bombing."

"The Sodality?" Weston said.

"Bingo, that's the whole kielbasa," Shay said, pushing a shirt sleeve back to look at his wristwatch. "Look, detectives, I'm sorry. Agent Crockett and I have another meeting. Agent Wallingford will see you out."

After gathering papers for his next meeting, he stopped at Viola's desk. "I'll need your help right now. "You recall Professor Gordon of Marquette?"

She did, and yes she'd heard the sad news of his death and yes of course she'd be happy to find an address and inform Tom Weathering of the sad news. Did Agent Shay want to write the message now? Shay did.

Later that night at home, Shay poured four fingers of Scotch into a Waterford tumbler and sat down on his sofa. He drummed his fingers on the coffee table, running through his options for tracking Mira Borja down. Interpol? Too bureaucratic. Vatican Bank? Too loyal to the Sodality. His sociable Siamese sprawled across one side of his desk, pawing at the travel page of the Milwaukee Sentinel. Shay saw an advert for a budget round trip fare from Milwaukee to Frankfurt. An idea stirred in his mind. The Agency owed him three weeks of vacation. Maybe a working vacation?

With a stopover in Germany to debrief Tom and Chiara on Mira and the Sodality. All off the books. All unofficial. He'd need a civilian sidekick to provide cover for his snooping around the case oversees. Maybe Joseph Terwilliger now that he'd cashed out of the Spudnut Shop and had money to burn.

Chapter Twenty-Three

Göttingen. February 1967.

Chiara was glad they'd bracketed the topic of Mira while they made their apartment habitable again and planned the move to Heidelberg. She was also sure that Mira would reenter their lives soon enough.

One evening, with the Göttingen apartment nearly livable, Chiara sank into a cane rocker next to Tom who'd already dropped into a salvaged recliner. "Almost done, maybe another day or two," she said to Tom, running a hand over the crown of her head. "Took weeks to clean up the mess. Not that the place feels like home again. But it'll do till we move to Heidelberg." She looked at Tom with a quiet air of authority and warmth. "You know it's for the best that we move, right?"

Tom reached for the bottle of Lambrusco that stood on a side table. He held it up to the window light. The amber glass twinkled with emptiness. "Rats, not enough left to wet a thimble."

"Hey," Chiara said again, "It's for the best, right?"

"Yes, of course," he said. "It's just that it goes against

the grain to cut and run."

"I know, but there are three of us to think about."

Tom stood up and stretched. "Right now there are only two of us since Mutti has Faith until three."

"Don't even go there! We've got some walls to repaint. Now get to work."

Tom leaned into Chiara, kissed the tip of her nose, and said, "I love you. You've nearly killed yourself putting our home back together. I wasn't all that much help, was I?"

"You did what you could. Zimmer's pushed you hard to wrap up your work here."

Chiara rocked back, closing her eyes to shut out the past two weeks that nearly brought her down after the break-in. The sweeping up of dish and glass shards. The hauling of replacement bed frames and nightstands from Mutti's attic. A nasty quarrel with a workman over a bill for shattered windows. What still hung in the air was some heavy lifting around the topic of Mira. But they'd put Mira on hold. Thank God. She'd need more strength and a clearer head to deal with that problem.

While they sheltered with Mutti after the break-in, she'd fallen into bed, bone-tired and fighting off a riddling anxiety about putting their friend to so much trouble. When fretting over Mutti didn't keep her wide-eyed, she winced at the thought of moving to Heidelberg, of turning Faith's life upside-down again, of settling into a new home while Tom finished up his semester in Göttingen. And their safety while separated from each other. She didn't dare go down that rabbit hole.

What's more, Tom's Göttingen fellowship ended at the

end of the term. After that they had no income unless her childhood friend Anita came through. She'd written Anita, asking for help finding an elementary school position on the Heidelberg Army base. Good old Anita. She'd promised to do her best. Over the years, they'd written each other. And now in a couple of months she'd see her friend face-to-face. There was so much to talk about. How had Anita coped with the abuse in parochial school? Still a Catholic? Did Anita enter a recovery program like she and some of the other girls had done? Was there a man in her life?

And then there was their host family in Heidelberg—the Dabelsteins—to worry about. A childless couple, according to Zimmer. Frau Dabelstein von Schubert was a baroness (God! Not another sketchy European aristocrat in their lives), her husband a senior theology professor at the university. Zimmer called them "good people" and war heroes (funny that, to think of Germans as war heroes). He had sprinted for Germany in the 1936 Berlin Summer Olympics. Then came the war and a decade of internment in a Russian gulag. With Zimmer and Wilhelm. But what did she really know about the character of these people? Nothing really. At the moment, they seemed like empty ciphers. Would they, could they, help feed, clothe, and house a quasi-refugee family, much less protect them against the Sodality? That was a lot to ask of total strangers. Ever cheerful Zimmer made it sound like the most natural thing for his colleague to do. She nearly choked on a cocktail of fear and doubt.

The rocker rails creaked as she leaned forward and

stood up to walk to the replacement patio door. A Macy's Christmas window came to mind as she looked over the snow that blanketed the shrubs and trees in the backyard all the way to Mutti's fence. In the swales between the crests of snow, spearheads of early crocuses and daffodils poked up defiantly. A Flemish rabbit hopped by, nibbled at a crocus, and moved on. Next door, Frau Kopp, the rabbit's owner, cursed out a window at her runaway pet. Chiara turned to Tom. "I'm going to miss this neighborhood. But not the drama." She checked her wristwatch. "Tom, you have a lecture at three." The empty wine glass drooped in her hand.

"I know."

"Clean up, and I'll walk with you to the tram stop and then collect Faith. Wonder if she's hungry?"

Faith was and begged for "zula." Settling the child at a table with a coloring book, Chiara put water on to boil and mixed an egg dough. Rolling the dough out evenly on a board, she took a sharp knife to cut pinky-lengths of spaetzle into the water. Ten minutes later, Faith dug into the buttery noodles with gusto. She only looked up from her "zula" when the metal flap on the mail slot creaked. Letters and flyers spattered across the floor. The doorbell rang. Chiara got up from the table to open the door.

"Special delivery, Frau O'Keeffe," said the postman. "Sign here." He handed her a small box wrapped in oilskin cloth and addressed to Tom. It was the size of a double deck of playing cards. Chiara bent over to gather up the mail then returned to the dining table. A chubby hand grasped for the package.

"Mine!" Faith said, leaning forward.

"No, darling. For Papa." Chiara turned the box over in her hands then moved it to the center of the table out of Faith's reach. She recognized the return address—the monastery in Venice. Hmm. What had they left behind? For several minutes, Chiara toyed with the food on her plate, dabbed at butter on Faith's chin. Pretending to ignore the box wasn't easy. Finally, curiosity won over. She picked the box up, gave it a shake. "What's inside, Faith?" she teased.

"Benice candy."

"Ha! I bet you're right. Candy from Venice." Chiara's imagination began to vamp. A gift from Tom, making up for his tawdry behavior in Venice? Or an anniversary gift? They'd been together a little over four years now. Wouldn't it be just like Tom to splurge on her with a sparkling piece of jewelry? She put the package back on the table and read the letters.

In one, Joseph Terwilliger wrote about booking a grand European tour and a side trip to Göttingen. In the other, Tom's high school classmate Mike Mathis grumbled about his new duty station near Heidelberg and invited himself for a weekend. She stared goggle-eyed at both letters, wondering how in God's name to welcome two guests just as they planned to pull out of town. Neither of the men had the sense to give a date. She puzzled over Mike's mention of a place called Rattlesnake Mountain. Where the heck was that?

Actually, it would be cool to see Joseph again and

meet Tom's childhood friend. She'd seen photos of Mike and Tom in a high school yearbook. In one the boys posed with the tennis team, both cracking wide smiles, full of swagger, and leaning on the net. She still pictured Mike's long muscular legs, cropped hair that bristled like a wire brush, and a broken nose. Handsome was not a word that came to mind. Perhaps angular and dangerous.

"Stories?" Faith asked, pulling at the letter.

"Well, sort of. Friends are coming to play. Good news for your daddy." But stressful news for her mommy. If those two men showed up at the same time, she'd have to cobble meals together for three men on a graduate student budget. Not to mention a few cases of beer. And right in the middle of their move to Heidelberg.

The package on the table caught her eye again. Chiara picked it up, gave it a shake, and heard a solid object rattle inside the box. That settled it. A surprise gift. She and Faith would make a special occasion out of dinner. True, it was just the usual *Abendbrot*—open-faced sandwiches. She'd dress it up with a can of peaches and a bottle of white Piesporter wine she'd set aside for a special moment. And to give the dinner a smidgen of romance, she'd spray herself and Faith with the last of her precious Arpège.

In Faith's room, they sprang into action, collecting scissors and crayons together with red and green colored paper. Tonight, they'd dress the dinner table with homemade placemats and flower cutouts. Sitting next to each other cross-legged on the floor, they cut out daisies, pasting them onto the sheets of paper. An hour later, Chiara pushed herself up with a groan. "So, now it's time for us ladies to dress." She reached for Faith's best tights and smock.

"Papa lub 'em, flowers," Faith said, as Chiara fastened a blue bow onto a curly lock of hair.

"For sure, darling. Papa lub 'em." Chiara slipped on a mod skirt and cashmere sweater. She twirled in front of Faith. "What do you think? Not bad, huh? Not bad at all. Despite two years nursing you, I've kept a figure. Don't pay any attention to the hint of crow's feet around my green eyes."

"Mama got grey hair," Faith said.

"A little Clairol will fix that," Chiara said to the child, as she glided madder red lipstick over her mouth, blotted, then touched up. She felt ready to overwhelm Tom, and she'd go up against Mira anytime, that scrawny, conniving scrap of cannoli. "OK, darling. We look beautiful. Let's cut some bread and cold cuts for our dinner. We'll put the little package next to Papa's plate.

That evening, when Tom arrived home, Chiara and Faith twirled him around the dinner table, making a point of the placemats and flowers. Each took a little curtsy as he oohed and awed over the table dressing and their outfits. Chiara seated Faith in her highchair and passed the platters of bread and cold cuts around. She told Tom about the two letters. "So, what if our friends both show up at the same time?" Chiara asked between bites. "We've only got three plates!"

"Mutti's got extra, don't you think?" Tom said, as he opened the wine and filled their glasses. "So, tell me, my darling ladies, what's all the fuss—?" Faith cut him off with a finger jab at the small package next to her plate.

"Wow, what's that?" He picked the package up and gave it a gentle shake. The contents rattled. Faith raised herself up in the chair.

"Probably nothing," Chiara said, trying to act causal even as she pinched an earlobe, feeling for a pierced hole, ready to receive a gold stud or even a dangle.

"Well, go ahead. Open it. It's from the monastery."

"Monastery?" Tom repeated, scrunching his eyebrows. "Not expecting anything."

Chiara played along. "Maybe you left a cufflink. Hee hee."

"No, Benice candy," Faith corrected.

Tom cut the twine around the package. The oilskin flaps opened to show a clamshell case. Chiara recognized an embossed shield—the monastery's coat of arms, she guessed—glittering back from the top of the case. She leaned into Tom as he stared at the contents. "What is it, Tom?"

Tom opened the case and tipped it toward Chiara. She gasped, hand flying to her mouth. A glittering gold bangle sparkled on a tuft of cream-colored silk. Three twisted gold cords formed a skein of serpent bodies. Pearls and diamonds filled each tiny cleft.

Chiara leaned forward for a better look and gave a whistle of surprise. "My God, for me?" Without waiting for an answer, she slipped the bangle on her wrist. Even in the half-light of the overhead lamp the bracelet glowed like a ring of fire. Slack jawed, she stared at Tom. "It's…too lovely…too heavenly…don't know what to say." Chiara turned the bracelet on her wrist, each rotation glittering with a new brilliance. "And a little scary too—the serpents." Her voice crackled with excitement. "I've never had anything so...so...dazzling."

"Want one," Faith said, reaching for her mother's arm.

"One day." She turned to Tom, waiting for the toothy grin that meant he'd pulled off a surprise. Instead, his forehead furrowed as he reached for a folded notecard in the bottom of the case.

Chapter Twenty-Four

Göttingen, February 1967.

"What's the matter with you," Chiara asked, her own brows knitted with confusion.

"I...I don't...get it," Tom stuttered. "I mean, it's from the monastery. But why jewelry? He looked up at Chiara. "We didn't leave anything behind. And the monks surely don't send thank you jewelry to their guests."

Why jewelry? Surely, she'd misheard Tom. Why not jewelry for a special occasion? Tom knew about the gold merchants on the Rialto Bridge. An upcoming anniversary. An apartment restored. A gesture to make the move to Heidelberg a little less daunting. "Well, what does the card say?" Chiara asked as she ripped the bangle off her wrist and slapped it down on the table.

Tom's face turned ashen. "This is crazy; I mean, it's from the abbot, Father Vartan. Can't be right."

Chiara snatched the card. "Dear Tom," she read, "What a lovely and productive time with you and your family. Enclosed is an item of jewelry that Chiara left under the bed. The community sends you fondest wishes for a blessed Lenten season. Faithfully yours in Christ, Father Vartan."

"Found under the bed? That's sure as hell's not mine," Chiara said, as she picked up the bangle and threw it at Tom's head. "Not mine! Do you flippin' understand?" She pushed back from the table, crimping the note in her hand, her eyes rounded, full of questions, smarting like hot coals. "Looks like Mira left something behind in the bedroom after your evening of...what did you call it? 'conversation'?" Faith started to whimper. She looked from her mother to her father then back again. Chiara covered her face with her hands, hiding the tears on her cheeks.

"Wait," Tom said. "I can explain. I mean, no, I can't explain. Please listen. It's not what you think." Tom's face went flush red. "It's not what you think."

"How do you know what I think?" Not what she thinks? Is that what Tom just said? She wasn't sure what she thought. Unseen spikes jabbed at her chest. Her head spun with thoughts that unspooled faster than she could catch them. Why did some men pretend to be one thing when they really were another? Was Tom one of those? No, he couldn't be, could he? She grasped the wine bottle by its neck, then let it go.

Chiara picked up the bread platter and flung it at Tom's head, narrowly missing him.

Faith cried, "No Mama, hurt Papa!"

Chiara swallowed a sob and swiped at the tears with her sleeve. "I love you and trust you. And you bed that loathsome woman and ruin our lives, our everything?"

Faith's eyes widened with fright. Her lips trembled.

"It's OK, baby," Chiara heard herself saying. "Papa and Mama have a booboo in their hearts."

She fixed her eyes on Tom, dragging herself back from the edge of fury. "Why haven't you come clean with me about Mira?"

"I screwed up by letting Mira into the apartment. We talked for an hour and finished a bottle of Hine. That's all I can remember of the evening. Except that she drugged me and got into my notebook and left me sprawled on a sofa. I remember the bangle…she wore it on her wrist."

Chiara couldn't keep it in any longer. "So did you have sex with her?"

"No. I mean, that's the part I don't know. I don't want to lie. That's God's truth. So much is a blank. I don't know."

Chiara pressed her face into her hands and sobbed. "How can such a smart guy be so stupid?" she said, "I should hate you for this."

"I'm sorry. Really sorry." Tom reached for Chiara's hand. She jerked it away. "Mira must've planted the bangle. She set me up. I'll figure it out. She's after something I didn't tell or show her."

Chiara's arched her eyebrows. Right, so what did Tom show the bitch that night?

"Give me time…please…to figure out what angle that woman's working, what this bracelet is all about. I've got a hunch she's a Sodality operative."

By now Chiara barely heard Tom and understood even less. Too exhausted from the cleanup and packing, she threw up her hands. "I'm going to need my own time to figure out what Faith and I do."

"Mama," Faith said, banging on the table with a spoon. "No cry, Mama. Happy girl."

Without a word she ran to their bedroom, threw clothes in a backpack, then picked up Faith and ran to the child's room. She locked the door and packed a suitcase for her daughter. Tom banged on the door, "Chiara, please give me a chance. We can figure it out. Please let's talk. I know what it looks like. Let me try to explain. Please. This is all wrong."

With a hard click Chiara unlocked the door, brushed past Tom, pushing him out of the way. She turned around. Words mingled with sobs. "Has loving a man…made me a fool…again? Why…do I feel it has? I'm afraid…to trust my feelings for you now." Without waiting for Tom to speak, she flung open the door to the apartment. "We're going back to Mutti's."

Tom hovered in the doorway. "Faith, take care of your Mama. Make her dress warm."

"Lub you Papa. Me keep Mama warm."

Running more than walking around the block to Mutti's, and not even ringing the door bell, Chiara burst into the living room, holding Faith in her arms. "May we come in?"

"Goodness, child," Mutti said, looking up. "You just gave me a scare. I didn't hear you open the back door." She sat on a sofa, knitting, her legs buried under a warm flokati blanket. In her practiced hands, the long shafts of her needles clacked as they held then dropped their stitches. The arm of a teal blue sweater fell row by row onto her lap.

On a low table in front of the sofa a fresh pot of lavender tea steamed in its padded cozy. Mutti dropped the knitting into her lap.

"Of course, my child," Mutti said. "Put your suitcases by the stairs." She gestured toward the sofa and settled her two guests on either side of her. Pulling the blanket over their laps, she handed Faith a small sweet from a box on the table. "So," she said, stabbing the needles into a skein of yarn, "have you and Tom quarreled? I wondered if the stress of the break-in and Project would be too much. My dear husband never knew how hard the burdens of his work fell on me."

"May Faith and I spend a few more days here?"

"By all means. Phil and Anna left this morning. There are clean sheets on their bed."

"Tom needs some quiet time, we're just in his way." For the moment she could offer nothing better to account for their sudden arrival. The earth had just opened and swallowed her whole.

The next morning, through a gap in the curtains of her bedroom window, Chiara snatched glimpses of Tom at his desk. That night, she saw him again, more shadow than substance, move about the sunroom, now plucking up a book, now filing some papers. The next evening, with the wind clattering the roof tiles, she saw him stand up and look toward her window. The thought of their eyes meeting drove her back into the shadows.

By midweek, more guilt than anger trickled through her heart. Had she turned into a hive of paranoia and jealousy, naive about the ways of men, imposing herself on a neighbor for shelter and comfort? What about Faith? What had she done to her daughter by running away from their apartment? She could only imagine. Twice Faith opened the backdoor and tried to walk across the snow to the fence. "Papa sick" and "help Papa" Faith said each time Chiara brought her crying daughter back to Mutti's house.

On the fourth day, when Tom showed up to make a phone call, Chiara listened from the second-floor landing while Tom spoke with Zimmer. A few minutes later, she saw him leave, carrying a basket of sandwiches and two bottles of beer. That night, sitting on the sofa with Mutti, she watched her knitting needles do their orderly work. Then suddenly she could hold her pain in no longer. She gulped in air as she poured out the story of Mira Borja. How she'd turned up in Venice. Clawed her way into their lives. Left a bangle under their bed.

When Mutti finally spoke, it was at first only about how thin Chiara and Tom looked, how Faith had sniffles, how little Tom must know about fixing for himself.

"Mutti, have you not heard a word I said?" Chiara asked, her voice cracking, eyes drizzling tears.

"Oh, yes, my dear, I have," she said, stretching out the sleeve of the sweater. "Do you think this will fit Tom?" She laid the sleeve down and reached for Chiara's hand.

"Fit Tom? Don't know. Not sure I care just now."

"Of course, you feel that way about Mira. About Tom, too. What female hasn't wanted to rip the eyes out of a woman making a play for her man?"

Chiara's whole body trembled, and Mutti wrapped an

arm around her shoulder.

"Think of this though," Mutti said, picking up her skein of yarn. "A sleeve is only part of a sweater. There is much wool yet to unravel and knit into the garment. Hard to know what the whole piece will look like until it is finished.

Chiara shook her head. "Why are we talking about a sweater? I'm trying to keep my family from falling apart."

"Oh, Chiara. It's the way of old women to speak in stories and riddles. I'm saying that knitting a sweater is like building a family. Each comes together and then one day stays whole. But only after some dropped stitches, some hard knots, even some unraveling. Give Tom time to sort out what happened. There is surely more to this story."

"Well, to me the thing looks pretty done. That bracelet came from under our bed in the monastery. And I sure didn't leave it there."

"I know you didn't. But that doesn't mean Tom betrayed you with that woman."

Chiara chewed on her lower lip. "OK. So what does it mean?"

"I think it means that Tom did something foolish and that he's about to pay a price for his foolishness. But one evening's folly doesn't unravel you two, much less the Project. I have watched you, Tom, and Faith. Love centers your family, and that center will hold no matter what. As long as you two stay together and work things out. You hurt terribly, and want to hurt back. This I can tell you. Mira brought evil to Venice, and into the apartment that night."

"So, what should I do?"

"Don't rush to judgment. Truth will come out. In its time. You must be patient with each other. And now you must go to bed."

Chiara threw her arms around Mutti's neck. "Thank you for talking with me." On the way upstairs she wondered if she felt any better. Possibly. At least she wouldn't fall asleep thinking about putting a gun to someone's head.

The next morning, while Faith slept, Chiara dressed and tiptoed out of the room. Pausing at the top of the staircase, she heard Mutti talking on the phone in the downstairs hallway.

"…yes…of course, Professor Zimmer. I will be happy to give Tom the message. Ten a.m. tomorrow, at your fencing club, the *Corps Hannovera*, right?"

Chiara took the steps two at a time and turned the corner into the hallway just as Mutti hung up the phone. "Message for Tom?" There was a hitch of excitement in her voice.

"He meets Zimmer at 10 a.m. tomorrow morning at his fencing club. Here's the address. A large package from Venice arrived. Would you like to tell Tom? There's a dress code. Tom will want a jacket and tie."

Chiara bolted out the door. She found Tom in their kitchen, stirring a cup of NesCafé. "Hi," she said, trying to measure out the thinnest possible smile.

Tom put his cup down on the counter and took a step forward. "Hi. Wow, what a surprise. Just made a cup of coffee. Join me?"

Chiara swallowed an urge to say yes. "No thanks. You have a message from Professor Zimmer."

"What's up.?

"Package from Venice. Meet him tomorrow at—." She forgot the German word Mutti had used. "—at his club. Ten sharp."

"Club? You sure? Not the office? That's weird."

"Here's the address." She handed him a slip of paper.

"The photographs of the papyrus fragments from the laboratory in Venice must have arrived. Tom held up his cup of coffee toward her. "You sure? Wanna come with me to Zimmer's club?"

"No, and No. Not quite ready," she fibbed. "Oh, Mutti said jacket and tie."

"I've climbed the fence a couple of times. Wanted to see you and talk. Mutti sent me packing. I'm pretty helpless without you and Faith."

Chiara laughed. "Good for Mutti. She's been my guardian angel all week."

"You look great. I miss you so much." He reached for Chiara's hand. She pulled back. "How's Faith?"

"Misses you. Look, I have something to say. I shouldn't have run away from this problem after I saw the bracelet."

"I'd love to see her—just for a hug?"

"Tom, did you hear what I said about running away?"

"Yes. Sorry."

"Just this. Running away I left Faith and myself in a bad place. I should've stayed and duked it out with you instead of letting you sweep things under the carpet. It's been a terrible week for us."

"I know. For me too. And I'm ashamed about the stupid evening with Mira. Please forgive me. I'll make it up to you. So, can I see Faith?"

No, not now," Chiara blurted then regretted the harsh tone. "Maybe...depends." Two telegrams on the counter caught her eye.

"Came today," Tom said, handing the telegrams to Chiara. "Remember the letters we got last month from Tom and Joseph. Well, both guys plan to visit us this weekend. And with this mess." He swept a hand around the room. "A pickle, them both visiting at the same time." He scratched his head as if a solution lay hidden in his hair.

"Mutti's got extra table settings. I could help finish up the cleaning, I suppose. You'd see Faith that way."

"Really, you'd do that?" Tom sounded genuinely taken aback. "Thanks."

For an instant, they were a perfect couple again— warm, excitable, tight. "Where're they staying?"

"Gebhards Hotel." Tom stared at his shoes for a long moment. "Thanks for giving me a chance to sort things out."

"You're welcome. And I'm going to need time, too." Chiara ran her hand over Tom's stubbled growth of whiskers. How can you want to throttle a man and kiss him at the same time? She missed his laughter and tenderness, their shared stories of Faith's capers, their pillow talk, their legs coiled in bed like a Celtic knot, and—only God knew why—the adrenaline rush of matching wits with the Sodality.

Her eyes must have betrayed her thoughts. Tom pulled her into his arms, and for a long moment an unexpected tremor of pure desire swept her away.

Chapter Twenty-Five

Göttingen, February 1967

Tom stepped off the tram at *Bürgherstrasse*, bucking a cold wind as he headed toward Number 58, the house address that Mutti wrote down for Zimmer's fencing club. Five minutes later, he reached a barred entrance gate and looked through its wrought ironwork. My God. What a spread, was all he could say.

Jutting up from a wide brown lawn rose a gaudy three-story mansion that horseshoed over the property and rippled in shades of orange and brown. Towers, some crenelated, some spired, bristled with gargoyles and finials. A brass plate etched with a shield and two crossed swords read: CORPS HANNOVERA GÖTTINGEN.

Sheesh, maybe he'd gotten the address wrong. This building housed one of the university's legendary fencing fraternities. Then it hit him. Of course. Zimmer's scar. The old man fenced as a student. Well, now, the morning promised to be full of surprises. He rang a bell on the gatepost and identified himself into a speaker. An electric motor whirred. Tom passed though the stonework posts as the gate swung open At the front door, a porter met him before he could pull on a bell rope. "Yes?" he said in a voice so deep it seemed to come from under the earth.

Tom took a step back. "Is Professor Zimmer in? He's expecting me."

"The honorable fencing master awaits you in the senior master's parlor." He bowed and stepped aside to admit Tom. "This way, please." At the end of a hallway, the porter knocked on a door. "I'll leave you here."

"Come in, Tom," Zimmer said.

"Good morning, professor…er…what do I call you here?"

"I'm still your professor."

Inside, Tom turned in a full circle to take a measure of the room. Velveteen wallpaper glistened behind rack after rack of sparkling sabers, rapiers, and foils. The weapons looked as deadly as they did elegant. His nose puckered at a woody scent that filled the room. He knew the smell from Mutti's living room: bees wax. Here a housekeeper had slathered it on the three leather couches that encircled a coffee table. An open bottle of cherry schnapps waited on the table. Next to it was a fat, padded envelope bearing Italian stamps.

Zimmer sat in the sofa facing the door, puffing leisurely on a thick cigar. His flushed face blended into a black and red sash that crossed from shoulder to waist. Gold thread glittered on the piping that decorated his short jacket. A sword-handled cane—one Tom hadn't seen before— lay across the coffee table.

"Make yourself comfortable," Zimmer said affably.

With a hand already holding a half-full tulip glass Zimmer gestured toward the bottle on the coffee table. "Drink?"

"Bit early for me, sir." Tom settled into the sofa facing Zimmer. Over the professor's shoulder he saw two framed photographs. In one, a brash, young Zimmer, looking splendid in a Corps cap and jacket, brandished a saber. A scar angled down his right cheek. In the other, Tom recognized the hollow-eyed figure of an older Zimmer, peering out from behind the barbed wire of a Russian gulag.

Gesturing at the figure in a Corps cap and jacket, Tom said, "You look pretty lethal with that sabre in hand."

Zimmer blushed. "Yes. A privilege of youth to look so confident. I keep the gulag photo next to it. A reminder of how passing and fragile that youthful confidence turned out to be." Zimmer traced the scar on his face as if to polish the memory, then picked up the padded envelope on the table. "So, let's get to work," he said. "We can talk openly here. Not so much back on campus."

"Why the cloak and dagger stuff?"

"You'll see in a moment. Sure about the drink?"

Actually, an early morning snort sounded good. "May I top yours off?" Tom asked, reaching for the bottle, refilling Zimmer's glass and pouring one for himself.

Zimmer pushed the package across the table toward Tom. "We've got a problem, I think."

"How so?"

"You and Father Davit left the *Panarion* with a lab in Venice, right?"

Tom nodded his head. "With instructions to

photograph the papyrus fragments in the three envelope pages."

"And then?"

"To send the photographs directly to us here in Göttingen and return the *Panarion* to the monastery."

"Well, look at the return address on the package with the photographs. What do you see?"

"The address of the monastery not the university."

It took Tom a moment to understand. "No! Can't be." He nearly dropped his glass as his mind reeled through dark scenarios. What if Mira returned to the monastery after he left? Or never even left at all? What if Father Davit had handed copies of the photographs to Mira? No, impossible. He trusted the conservator. How long before the copies reached the Sodality? And how long before Sodality experts worked out that the Androgyne Papyrus lay hidden in the *Panarion?* The questions piled up. He'd need more than one drink to get through this morning.

He'd been too trusting, too naïve. He should have reckoned on a Sodality sympathizer or operative in the monastery. How else could Mira have shown up at the same time he and Chiara did? Who was pulling Mira's strings? Tom chanced a look at Zimmer. The old man looked sullen.

Zimmer's next remark read Tom's. mind. "I need to brief you on a man named Roberto Cavalier. He's better known as the head of the Sodality."

Abbot Roberto Cavalier put down the phone and chuckled. He looked at his housekeeper, Doña Manuela, who was dusting his bookshelves. "That was the Countess Miranda Borja. She tells me we have photographs of the lost letter. Well, photographs of the remaining Greek fragments. Thanks to Father Davit."

"What happy news for you, Beto."

The abbot rolled his eyes. Doña Manuela still called him by his childhood name. In her mind he was still a child. Truth was, he depended on Doña Manuela more than she knew. She saw to everything here in Rome. The upkeep of the apartment in the basilica of St. Mary Major. His diet, his exercise, his medications for heart disease. Thanks to her, he could still at sixty-five, cut a sharp figure with his wide shoulders, narrow hips, and dark eyes. That his neck was red-veined and his face tinged with a grayness—well, that was not her fault. He blamed a German professor named Zimmer and an American graduate student named Tom Weathering. He prayed the package from Mira Borja brought an end to this matter.

"The countess is a fine operative! Is that not so, Beto?" the old woman asked. "How did she secure these photographs?'

"The countess returned to the monastery for a few days after the Americans left. Father Davit gave her photographic proof that the remains of the lost letter lie inside the *Panarion's* envelope pages. Of course our own experts must confirm this finding. Once they do, we can move quickly to destroy the *Panarion* and remove this plague from our lives."

"You have done much good today, Beto. I set the table for your dinner guest tonight. Now you must rest."

"Not yet. I have work to do. I expect a courier to deliver the photographs this evening."

Doña Manuela shrugged her shoulders and shuffled into the dining room. Her hand cupped an arthritic hip, and she winced in pain. From his desk the abbot could hear the clinking and tinkling of flatware and tableware finding their place on the table.

"It is urgent that you bring the package to me as soon as it arrives," the abbot called out from his office.

Shortly before 8:00 p.m. the doorbell rang. A moment later Doña Manuela led Bishop Marcony, senior director of the Vatican Bank, into the abbot's study. She offered him a tumbler of Kentucky bourbon then a platter of squid and black olives. "I will serve dinner in thirty minutes," she said.

Over their drinks Abbot Roberto kept the conversation light. He asked about American football.

"Ever hear of Rudy Bukish?" Bishop Marcony asked.

"I'm afraid not."

"Quarterback for the Chicago Bears. Threw thirteen consecutive pass completions in the 1964 season."

Abbot Roberto nodded. "Here's one for you. Do you know the name of Italy's most famous soccer player?"

"Hell if I do."

"Gianni Rivera," Abbot Roberto said, pointing to a photograph of the player on his desk. "He's a national hero. His seven goals helped Milan win the *Coppa Italia.*"

Doña Manuela rang her silver dinner bell. Abbot Roberto guided his guest by the elbow into the dining room. Doña Manuela, unusually silent, served risotto followed by a veal scallopini and a side dish of green beans drizzled with lemon.

After dinner the abbot invited the bishop into his office where the two churchmen settled into oversized armchairs under a gold-paneled ceiling. Doña Manuela poured generous cognacs from a crystal decanter then brought out the abbot's cedar-lined humidor of Cuban Montecristos #2.

Abbot Roberto brought up the matter of the Banco Ambrosiano, which tax authorities in Italy had recently targeted as subject of interest.

"Ah, the Ambrosiano," Bishop Marcony said. "Hmm. So you know about that?"

"Yes, the Sodality admires its work, especially the offshore investment it made available to the Vatican Bank." A highly illegal offshore investment.

The bishop drained his snifter, nodding for a refill. "Umberto Calvi, president of the Ambrosiano managed the transaction. Say...would you like to meet Calvi?"

"If it's not too much trouble." Abbot Roberto tried to sound only mildly interested. Truth was the Sodality urgently needed funds. The expenses for recovering the lost letter had shot wildly out of control. And then there was the matter of dealing with Tom Weathering and Professor Zimmer. God only knew what silencing them might cost.

The men sniffed and sipped their cognac in an easy silence, Abbot Roberto envisioning a loan of 10,000,000 Lira, Bishop Marcony cocking his head at an abstract oil in blue tones that hung on a wall. "Helluva painting that one," the bishop said. "Looks like a pair of horse butts."

"That's Franz Marc's *Blue Horses.*"

"Horses, you say? Well, I'll be jiggered." The bishop pulled out a checkbook from his jacket. "I play the ponies in Chicago. How much you want for those horses?"

"I'm afraid it's not for sale."

The doorbell rang. A moment later Doña Manuela glided into the study and held out a package. "A man of the post office leaves this for you. From Venice. And so late as to contract my sleep."

Somehow Doña Manuela always got the last gibe in. Never mind. He turned to his guest. "May I show you something?" Abbot Roberto asked.

"Later. The evening's young. We got a lot of your sauce to drink."

Abbot Roberto ignored the bishop and asked Dona Manuela to bring a pair of scissors from his desk. He cut the string and removed a dozen protectives sleeves covering glossy black and whites. To an untrained eye the photographs amounted to no more than a slurry of Greek letters without word breaks. To the abbot, however, who read Greek, they were enough to make his head whirl with excitement. Tomorrow he'd forward the photos to a manuscript expert in the Vatican Museum to confirm their content. His gut told him that Yes, by God! He had his proof—the envelope pages of the *Panarion* did indeed hold the remains of Apostle Paul's Letter to the Laodiceans. As soon as his manuscript expert confirmed this hunch, he'd send operatives to the monastery to secure the *Panarion* and bring it to Rome. He already itched to toss the cursed book into the hulking furnace in the basement of the cathedral. But first he needed to bait the bishop with the photographs.

"I have a favor to ask," the abbot said to the bishop. "With these photographs, I can complete an important mission. I can explain the matter if you wish."

"Nah, you're the expert." The bishop blew out a funnel cloud of cigar smoke in the direction of the painting. "What'dya need from me?"

"There are expenses involved. Rather heavy outlays of cash if I am going to prevent the writing in these pictures from harming our Catholic faith. I need more operatives in Italy and Germany. Especially Germany. I must keep eyes on Professor Walther Zimmer and Tom Weathering in Göttingen."

"If it's funds you need, well just say so, man," the bishop said, draining his glass and thumping it down on a side table. "How much you say for those horse butts?"

Chapter Twenty-Six

Göttingen, February 1967

"Let's order some coffee while you tell me about the abbot and the Sodality," Tom said. "The alcohol's gone to my head."

Zimmer buzzed for a steward. "While we wait," he said, "look at the wax seal on the back of the envelope, Tom. It's a fake." There was a sharp edge to his voice. "Someone in the monastery opened the envelope, probably copied the photographs, and then resealed it."

"That's not possible," Tom said." Yet even as he said this, his gut told him it was. Mira had gotten hold of the photographs.

"Oh, but it is. Take a look at this." Zimmer pulled a circular magnifying glass from a briefcase and held it over the seal. "Look closely at the wax impression. What do you see?"

"A shield embossed with a cross. And, in each of the quadrants of the cross, a symbol—a flame, a bell, an open book, and a walking stick." There was a knock on the door and a grave-looking steward entered.

Zimmer ordered a pot of coffee then, heaving himself up from the sofa, crossed the room to a bookcase. He reached for a book entitled *European Heraldry*. He flipped through the volume, stopping at a page marked with a slip of paper. Returning to the sofa, he said, "The official seal of the monastery shows a shield embossed with a cross. "Do you see the four symbols that run around the quadrants of the cross?"

"Same symbols. Different order."

Zimmer closed the book and dropped it heavily on the table.

"I screwed up," Tom said, his face loaded with gloom. He looked at a large globe in the corner of the room. He wanted to run and hide behind it. "Sorry, sir. Seemed a good plan at the time, to leave things to Father Davit to handle. I'll make it right. You can bank on that."

"Look, you couldn't have known that the Sodality owned Father Davit. *Scheiss* happens." He raised his glass, touched Tom's and said, "Let's keep moving." Zimmer opened the envelope and lifted out three black and white photographs, spreading them out across the table. Each photograph showed one or more papyrus fragments with columns of Greek words written across a lined surface. "So, these are the photographs that the university made after they scanned the contents of the envelope pages."

Zimmer arranged the photographs side by side on the table. "Did you bring Sona Routanian's translation?"

"Yes," Tom said, glad he'd done one thing right that morning. He began to arrange the pages of Sona's translation in a row above the black and white photographs.

"So, if we are right," he said, "the Greek text of the Venice university photographs should more or less line up word for word with Sona's English translation of the Armenian."

Tom read the first line of Sona's translation. "Paul the Apostle to the church in Laodicea. Grace and peace."

Zimmer's head nodded as he followed the Greek words in the photograph. "Matches up. Keep going."

"In Christ there is neither Jew nor Greek, slave nor free, male nor female."

"Good," Zimmer said. Now look at the last sheet of fragments, where Paul signed off on the letter. You know he probably dictated the letter to a scribe, right?"

Tom nodded and turned to the last sheet. He translated a list of greetings to members of the Laodicean church. Then he came to Paul's well-known signature. "I, Paul, write this greeting with my own hand. I sign off with my usual big letters."

"That sounds like the end of other letters Paul dictated and then signed, right?" Zimmer asked. "I think you've found the lost Letter to the Laodiceans, your Androgyne Papyrus."

"*We* have. And it's safely tucked inside the envelope pages of the *Panarion*," Tom said, his blood rising in a jet and letting out a loud whoop. "Sir, there is one more thing to tell you."

"One more thing?" Zimmer said.

"Well, ah…" It took Tom ten minutes to get out his story of a cognac-fueled evening with Mira Borja, the drug, the bangle, the falling out with Chiara. When Tom finished, Zimmer reached for his silver-headed walking stick, stood up, and limped to the globe. He spun the orb in its cradle then gave it a hard whack with his stick. "What happened between you and Mira Borja is something that you and Chiara must sort out. Don't do wrong by your good woman."

"I know sir. I'm trying hard to repair the mess."

"As far as I'm concerned," Zimmer said, "there is an immediate threat to the Papyrus. Abbot Roberto and his henchmen will stop at nothing to lay hands on the *Panarion* and destroy the envelope pages, maybe even the whole codex."

Zimmer spoke in a low voice that Tom recognized as sadness if not resignation to the fate of the Papyrus. The old man's helplessness galvanized Tom. He jumped up and joined Zimmer at the globe. "Like hell the Sodality will get the goods," he said. "No, sir. Not going to happen. I know I've let you down. But I've got my second wind and am ready to join the fight with the Sodality again." Tom walked around the globe as if planning a great strategy. He felt a surge of adrenaline and plunged ahead as if he were the professor and not the student.

"Here's what I think we need to do, sir." You call the abbot, Father Vartan. Tell him to put the Armenian codex under guard. Sleep with it if he must. Chiara and I'll take a train to Venice next Monday and bring the *Panarion* here."

Zimmer shook his head. "I'm not sure Tom."

"Wish I could go earlier. Can't though. Friends arrive this weekend."

"The monastery will never release the *Panarion* to you."

"Oh yes, it will. You put your weight behind my request. The abbot respects and trusts you and owes you a debt for the care you took of the old monk in the gulag so many years ago. You sat a deathwatch with the old man. Gave him a Christian burial. That's got to be worth a lot to the abbot."

"I'll call Abbot Vartan and see what I can do. If we're not already too late."

A steward walked in to clear the coffee. He handed Zimmer a note. "It's a message for your guest from Chiara." Zimmer gave the sheet of paper to Tom.

"Yikes, looks like our guests have arrived. My childhood friend Mike Mathis and another guest from Milwaukee, Joseph Terwilliger."

Chapter Twenty-Seven

Göttingen. February 1967.

US Army Sergeant Mike Mathis stepped up to the front desk of the Hotel Gebhards, unslung his backpack, and eased it to the floor. He held out a passport and military ID for the clerk, a sleepy, rumpled man with one sleeve of his jacket pinned to his chest. The clerk glanced back and forth from Mike's photo ID to his faded Levis, *Jefferson Airplane* sweatshirt, and bush jacket. "Here, look at this," Mike said, reaching into a jacket side pocket for a weekend pass that gave him three days off base to visit his childhood friend, Tom Weathering. He wondered if the old man had lost the arm in the war and resented the US soldiers now stationed in Germany. Be nice to chat up the guy if he had a minute.

The clerk squinted at the paperwork then pushed the hotel ledger across the counter toward Mike. "Sign here, *bitte*," he said. He handed Mike a room key dangling on a chain and bronze globe. "The other *Amerikaner* meets you in the bar at 6 p.m."

"Other American? Oh right. Thank you," Mike said.

He slipped a hand into a jean pocket and pulled out Tom's telegram: FAMILY FRIEND JOSEPH TERWILLIGER STOP ALSO AT GEBHARDS STOP. Sweet. He'd collect Terwilliger and invite him to dinner. Tom didn't plan to meet them till the next morning.

Grabbing his backpack, he headed for an elevator. Nearly six feet of rangy, powerful male, he had a broken nose and a crocodile smile. His buddies joked that he looked like a dude who could take a punch as well as crack a joke. At twenty-four he'd already served two tours in 'Nam, the last as an Army coxswain on one of the Navy's Mekong River patrol boats. He carried himself with the seriousness and humility that war gave to soldiers who walked out of a combat zone alive and whole.

When had he last seen Tom? Six years ago? More nearly seven. A lot of water under the bridge in that time. And now the guy had a family, so add a lady and a kid to the catching up. The last time he'd hung out with Tom, summer of '61, they'd just graduated high school. Then he blew off a full ride at UCLA to enlist in the Army. His folks went ballistic. The scene on the front porch of his home—his mother crying, his father leaning into him, ranting—still spooled through his head. "How could you be such a cotton-pickin' numbskull, boy? Tom's enrolled in engineering at Gonzaga and you...you're heading for Vietnam. Good luck with that."

Cripes. He swallowed hard over a sudden lump of sadness. Maybe one day he and Dad could sort it out. Meanwhile, he had a lot to catch up with Tom. Then there was Tom's mention of "Rattlesnake Mountain" in his invitation to come visit. What the hell was that about? Whatever. Should be a cool weekend especially if Tom kept a stash. He'd gotten used to toking anytime in 'Nam. On an American base in Germany not so easy.

The lift ground to a stop. The grate creaked open. Mike's foot sunk into a plush carpet that ran the length of a wide hallway. Good to be in civilization again, if only for a weekend.

In the room, Mike unpacked then showered until the hot water reservoir on the wall ran dry. At 6 p.m. sharp, dressed in khakis and a crew neck sweater, he locked his room and took the stairs to the first floor. In the low light of the nearly empty bar, he heard the clack of dice rolling along the polished surface. He sauntered up to a smartly dressed black man perched on a stool, snapping shut a dice boat. Mike stuck out a hand, "Guessing you're Joseph. Name's Mike."

"That's me," Joseph said, flashing a smile full of gold fillings. He swept up a pile of German Mark coins. "Just beat myself at craps," he said. "Pleased to meetcha. Any friend of Tom's a friend of mine." With a long pull on a drink, he drained his glass. "Whisky sour. Got a jump on ya, man. Hope ya don't mind. Needed a stiff one. Got tossed bad by German Customs in Frankfurt. Left me feelin' pretty hot."

"Sorry about that shit. The Kraut at the front desk didn't exactly warm up to me either when he saw my military ID. Must still be fightin' the war." He settled on a stool next to Joseph. "Hey, love the Marvin Gaye look," Mike said with a thumbs up for the man's glittery blue jacket.

"You pegged it, man. Ain't no mountain high enough..." Joseph fished for an ice cube in the bottom of his glass. "Tom's talked about you. You're a lifer, right?"

"Two tours in 'Nam. PBR skipper. Just re'd-up for a third. Stationed at Patton Barracks in Stuttgart."

"PBR?"

"Patrol Boat Riverine. Mekong Delta." He caught the eye of a bartender and flashed two fingers. "My round." While they waited for the drinks, Mike unlaced his tennis shoes and dropped them on the floor under the stool, propping his feet on a heated brass foot rail. "My dogs are barking. Not used to civilian shoes. Try it. One of the guys on base told me about these gizmos." Joseph slipped his loafers off. The men's faces rearranged themselves into a grin. "Nice, huh?"

Mike ordered a second then a third round of Whiskey Sours and filled the time with stories about growing up with Tom on the Columbia River, near Richland, Washington.

"Sure do miss that family," Joseph said. "Ever' Saturday like clockwork they showed up at the Spudnut Shop. Selling the Shop was the hardest thang I ever done."

Mike left that stone unturned. There was grief in the story. "You stay in touch with Tom and Chiara after they left for Germany?" Mike asked.

Joseph's hand rubbed a wide swath of scar tissue on his neck. "The church bombing left me that callin' card," he said. "Did I stay in touch? Fur a while. Then not so much. I was in a world of hurt. The bombin' took my good

friend Precious Dilbarton and our pastor, Father Grapiano."
Joseph took a long pull on his drink. "Not to mention
nearly killin' Tom, Chiara, and Faith."

"Cripes," Mike said," Sounds like the church was a
war zone. Sorry for the loss. Cops ever catch the bomber?"

"You kiddin'? Black church? Black neighborhood?
FBI jumped in. Fact is I tried to help the feds, informal like,
talkin' up folks in the neighborhood. Nuttin' much come of
it. Did get to know an FBI fellah named Henri Shay."

"Can't be easy. Precious gone, church a wreck, Shop
sold."

"Well, I tell you what I gotta live with," Joseph said,
one hand twirling ice in his glass. "It was me what invited
Tom and his family to Mass the day of the bombin'."

"Jesus," Mike said, putting a hand on Joseph's arm.
"You're not to blame."

"Still and all, I invited 'em."

"You look to be doin' OK now," Mike said. "Here you
are in Europe. Nice threads. No worries."

Joseph eased his drink down on the bar. There was a
long silence. Tom knew he'd pushed a wrong button. "I
ain't apologizin' for livin' high," Joseph said, his voice
thick with anger. "My place to do so."

"I never said it wasn't. Chill, man. It's cool." He held
up his glass to Joseph. "Bottoms up."

"You ain't got no reason to ride me hard," Joseph said
with a defiant lift of his chin. "After what went down at
church? Not that it's your business. Sold the Shop to some
Eyetalians. For more boodle than I ever seen. Got the hell
outta town. Been improvin' myself ever since."

Mike stared into his Whiskey Sour as if some bar wisdom might float to the surface. He'd had his own close calls in 'Nam. Like hitting a mine that the VC laid. Changes a fellah. Makes you see things different. You get shaky. You take on guilt for surviving. Carry baggage with you. But Joseph? Something didn't ring true in the dude's story. He sounded like a man who felt the opposite of survivor's remorse. Was there such a thing as survivor's reward?

Mike said, "Tom wrote about the bombing, the deaths, the damage to your church. I've seen that kinda shit firsthand in 'Nam. Me and my boat crew dropped acid and smoked pot to stay numb and sane. When we lost a buddy we hit the shit really hard. We all have holes in our lives, Joseph, some bigger than others."

Joseph turned to face Tom. "Cain't figger you, whether you dissin' me or not. You think I shoulda stayed back in the 'hood, slinging Spudnuts? That I ain't got a right to nice clothes, fat wallet, some respect from folks?"

Mike bit his tongue. But the whiskey talked. "You lost a pastor, a lady friend, a church. Tom, Chiara, and Faith nearly bought it, too. And God only knows how many other church goers." He took a long pull on his drink. "Just sayin' you moved on pretty fast."

A muscle in Joseph's face spasmed. "Now lookit here, mister, you got no idea what I bin hurtin'. You judgin' thangs you know nothin' about." Joseph slipped off the bar stool and stood next to Mike, towering over him. With a meaty hand he put a vice grip on Mike's shoulder. In a voice like the lowest register of an organ he said, "You gotta back off. Otherwise, you go home on a stretcher." Joseph unbuttoned his jacket, and Tom saw the rim of a shoulder holster.

"Easy brother," Mike said, slipping off his stool and taking a step back. The man wasn't dumb enough to pull a gun in a bar. But they were both drunk and could easily do something stupid. "Look, Joseph, let's stand down. For Tom's sake. I'm sorry. Empty stomach. Too much booze." He lifted Joseph's hand from his shoulder. "We're gonna spend a weekend together with Tom. Let's make the best of it."

"Fine by me," Joseph said as he sat down. "I'm a forgivin' man. Jes' don't meddle into thangs you know nuttin' about."

A shadow fell over the two men. "I can seat you now," said a waiter. He held out a gloved hand and guided them to a linen-covered table, fully set, with a view of the Old Town's lights.

Chapter Twenty-Eight

Göttingen, February 1967

Mike ordered a bottle of Chianti and two platters of starters. The men tucked hungrily into the buttery cheeses, Genoa salami, sweet pickles, and Black Forest ham. By the time the entrees arrived—breaded veal cutlets and roasted potatoes—the kerfuffle with Joseph had faded away.

"Amazed me," Mike said, motioning to a waiter for another bottle of Chianti, "that Tom settled down with a woman and had a kid. Never figured the guy for the marryin' type."

"More like Chiara ain't the marryin' type," Joseph said, swiping at a dab of sauce on his chin. "Heard that from Precious. Just livin' wid Tom suited her fine."

"Doesn't much matter. They're crazy about each other." Mike reached for his wallet and unfolded a black and white of Tom and Chiara. "Tom sent me this right after they met." He handed the photo to Joseph. A sloe-eyed lady looked right at the camera, head tilted, hair done in a French roll, and smiling so slightly it might not have been a smile at all.

"She's a looker," Joseph said. "Still is. Mind like a bear trap. Tom don't pull nothing on her." Joseph reached for his wallet and produced a crinkled shapshot. "That's my Precious." A smartly-dressed, middle-aged black woman with finger-waved hair gave a lazy, flirtatious smile.

"Nice looking lady. You must miss her."

"Suppose I do. We come close to tyin' the knot time or two. Wish I'd pushed harder. Ever' thang changed a lot for me after she passed. You got yersef' a woman?"

A flash of memory fractured Mike's composure and tossed him back in time. His arm prickled with Cam's touch as her fingers ran up and down his belly. He pictured playing with the kids, making love to her on a shaky cot, shopping in the open market. "Nah. Not anymore." He reached for his wallet again then knew there was no photo. She'd been camera shy. "For a few months in '65, I saw a local who worked as a translator in the American Embassy. Moved her and three kids into an apartment on the Ben Thanh Market. We were pretty tight. Truth was I knew she took up with me because of the kids. Then one day, she didn't show up for work. A Marine at the embassy told me local police had arrested her as a VC sympathizer. No way, I said…Oh hell, that's all in the past now." A wall clock struck 10 p.m. Mike pushed back from their table and yawned. "I'm worn flat."

"Nightcap in the bar?" Joseph asked. "Time change's killin' me."

"Sure. One for the road."

Mike led the way to the bar stools they'd filled two hours earlier. Joseph peeled off two twenties from a wad of cash. "Bottle of Canadian Club," he said to the barman. "Keep the change."

"What went down after the church bombing," Mike asked. "Tom didn't write so much after that."

"Well, I can tell you those kids had it rough," Joseph said. "First the church. Some bad burns. Then their friend Sona and her kids dropped out of sight. I think the threats to Professor Gordon pushed 'em over the edge. They changed. Watchful. Worried. And Chiara had the Eyetalian lady to worry about."

"Italian lady?"

The bartender clapped the whisky bottle and two glasses down on the bar. He scooped up the bills. "We close in thirty minutes," he said.

"Foreign student," Joseph said, "named Mira Borja. A countess or sumpin like that." Mike poured the whiskey. "Always figured she wanted to cut Tom out for hersef," Joseph said, lifting his glass and knocking down a big swallow. "Pretty lady and smooth talker. Gave hersef' aires. Could charm the skin off a snake."

"Cut Tom out? Nah. Fat chance if I know Tom's feelings for Chiara." Mike changed the subject. "What the hell was your church into that got it bombed? Tom and Chiara mixed up somehow?"

"The parish? Well, protests, marchin', that sorta thang. Cain't say for sure 'bout the kids. Thought you might know that."

"No, sorry." Dipping a hand into a bowl of cashews, Mike asked, "So, what brought you to Germany with all that...?" He caught himself before he ragged Joseph about his fat roll of bills. Whoa. Keep it light and easy. There was a side to Joseph that felt very off limits.

"I love those kids. They's like family to me." Joseph dabbed at an eye with a cocktail napkin. "They left without a real goodbye. I decided to look 'em up. Kept tellin' myself they had to be crazy to be here alone. And I gotta pal back in Milwaukee what wants to sightsee with me. That FBI fellah I mentioned. Gonna tour of some of them French wineries."

The ceiling lights flickered. "Time," called the bartender, wiping down the counters and collecting dirty glassware.

The next morning Mike found Tom at the front desk, chatting up the night clerk. He grabbed his friend by both shoulders, held him at arm's length then pulled him into a bear hug. "Jesus H. Christ, been too long. Can't hardly get my arms around your jelly roll."

"Well, you're not the beanpole I remember, either," Tom said. "You stealin' food from the chow hall?"

"You dumb ass, you've never eaten C rations or food from a field kitchen," Mike said. "Had a local lady who cooked a lot for me. God, it's good to see you."

"You and Joseph get together last night?"

"Yeah, we did. Dinner, drinks, lotsa rag chew about you and Chiara. Your ears ring? Almost blew the evening though. Shot my mouth off…"

"Hey, here's Joseph," Tom said, swinging around at the sound of footfalls, "Hey, man, you're a sight for sore eyes. You bring us a bag of day old Spudnuts?" He threw his arms around his friend.

"Jeepers, wish I coulda. Did bring you this." He handed Tom a gift bag. "Go ahead. Open it. Tom pulled the draw string and lifted out a tattered Milwaukee Braves cap.

"No, can't be. Professor Gordon's cap? Where'd you get it?"

"Yup, one and the same. 'Member Henri Shay the FBI agent? He took it from MPD after the cops released it from evidence. Asked me to give it to you."

Tom held the cap in his hands. "Boy, I miss Gordon. He didn't deserve to die that way."

"What happened? Mike asked.

"Long story short: some really nasty criminals killed him."

"Sorry for your loss," Mike said. "I guess you and Chiara were close to the man."

"You can say that," Tom said, putting the hat on his head and striking a batting stance. "Here's one over the fence for you, Gordon."

"Any leads on his killers?" Mike asked.

Tom shook his head. "Hey," he said, "I hope you guys ate a good breakfast. Full day ahead. Chiara doesn't want us till dinner. What do you guys want to see?"

By the time they'd finished sightseeing and arrived at Tom's apartment, it was nearly dark. Mike held a bouquet of irises—or at least its shaggy remains--in his hand. He'd stolen the flowers in the Botanical Garden.

"Mike, Tom's told me so much about you," Chiara said, throwing open the front door. "Feels like I've known you forever. She wrapped one arm around Mike's waist and took the flowers from his hand. "Come in. They're just lovely. I'll find a vase." She turned to Joseph, her eyes lighting up. "God, a face from the States. So good to see you, Joseph." She kissed Tom and closed the door behind the men.

"So, who's this little girl?" Mike asked as Faith toddled into the hallway, head cocked at the noise and holding a piece from a wooden puzzle. "Me Faith. I be berry busy." She gave a little curtsey and offered a tiny hand to Mike.

Joseph stepped up. "'Member me from the Spudnut Shop?" he asked. The child frowned then leaped into Joseph's arms. "Unca Joe," she cried.

"Let's eat," Chiara said, "before things go cold." She guided the men to the table and seated them on folding chairs. "Our friend, Mutti, sent over the platters of sauerkraut and bratwurst along with a basket of black bread and hard rolls."

"May I serve the wine?" Mike asked, reaching for the two pitchers on the table.

"Please do. Also from Mutti," Chiara said. "She keeps casks of red and white wine in her cellar.

Mike grasped a pitcher in each hand and overfilled the glasses, slopping wine on the table. "Oops, sorry. Bad shot. Big day today." Truth was he couldn't keep his eyes off Chiara. Lucky guy that Tom. The two of them had found their groove. She seemed open hearted, funny, smart. Maybe he'd get lucky one day. "Sorry for the mess," he said, dabbing at the spilled wine with a napkin. "Your guy totally wore us flat with a visit to campus, the Old Market, and the City hall. And then a long walk through the Botanical Gardens. What a sweat bath that place is."

For the next few minutes, the three men ate hungrily while Chiara and Faith talked about their day. "Faith and I read some books and cleaned out her toy box. And then it took us forever to make a cherry torte. A first for me," she said, forking up a mouthful of sauerkraut. "Thank God Mutti stopped by and gave us a hand."

"Me help, too," Faith chipped in.

"Joseph," Chiara said, "I hope you enjoyed the time with Tom and Mike. We miss Milwaukee so much."

"It was swell," Joseph said. 'Cept for the part when Tom buys us beers and preaches to us. Sumthin' about envelope pages and pieces of a crumbly old writing inside those pages. 'Bout all I caught was you movin' to Heidelberg. On account of all that old stuff. Sweet. You'll almost be neighbors to Mike."

"Oh, Tom, no," Chiara said, choking on a forkful of bratwurst. She clapped a hand to her mouth and shot Tom a withering look. "Zimmer told us to keep our plans to ourselves for a while."

"Sure," Tom said. "But Mike and Joseph are friends."

Chiara shook her head. A painful silence gripped the table. Finally, Faith broke in with "How come quiet time?" and set off a nervous laughter.

Chiara pushed back from the table. "Will you men please excuse Tom and me? He needs to help me cut up the dessert torte in the kitchen."

"Dessert?" Mike said. "God, I've not had homemade

pie in years," Mike said. "I'll never fit into my uniform after this meal. Cup of coffee, too, would suit me fine."

"Say," Tom said, standing up to follow Chiara into the kitchen. "We're going to Mass tomorrow. Guys wanna join us then find breakfast in the city? Afterwards Chiara and I gotta pack."

"Papa 'n Mama go to Benice," Faith offered. "Me stay with Mutti."

"No, thanks," Mike said. "Got an early train. You, too, Joseph. Right?"

"Venice?" Joseph said. "Sweet Jesus. I gotta see Venice. My Eurorail Pass's good for three months. How 'bout I tag along? I'll pay my way, and then some. Count on me for mass. I'll get a refund on my ticket to Norway."

Chiara clenched her jaw and exchanged a helpless look with Tom. Mike's heart sank. He gave Joseph a kick under the table. The man didn't take the hint. God. After cleaning up a wrecked apartment Tom and Chiara had earned a little private Venice time. He tried again to derail Joseph. "Hey, bro, thought you were traveling the other direction," he said. "Norway or Sweden."

"Sure, Joseph, why not?" Chiara said. "We'd love to have you along, right, Tom? Tell us all about the Spudnut Shop and the old neighborhood. I'll show you around the city. Lived there as a student." She pinched Tom's arm. He winced. "Help me serve the torte, mister."

A half an hour later, Mike pushed away from the table. He'd eaten well and loved the time with his friends. But worry pinged his chest. Joseph had hijacked Tom and Chiara's well-earned get-away. And there was nothing he could do to help. At the front door, Chiara handed him his parka. A smile flickered on her mouth.

"Nice try," she whispered. "It's OK. Tom's got his hands full at the monastery. Joseph will be good company. Good night. I've got to give Tom an earful for shooting off his mouth about Venice." She kissed him lightly on the cheek. "Thanks for taking the time to visit us. Meant a lot to Tom."

Mike felt a small lump in the parka's vest pocket. He reached inside the coat and fingered a small, aluminum wrapped packet. Thank you, Chiara. He'd put the hash to good use tonight. Tom probably would need a toke more than he did after Chiara took him down in the kitchen.

Chapter Twenty-Nine

Venice, February 1967

While the *vaporetto* steamed across the lagoon toward the monastery island, Tom tried to get Chiara's attention. He needed to talk things over with her one more time before they landed. But Joseph had wedged himself in the bucket seat between them. The guy had scored some weed when they changed trains in Munich. He'd gotten himself high and wound up, boasting about helping Agent Shay with the church bombing case.

Getting hold of the *Panarion* and bringing it to Zimmer still had too many loose ends. Checking things with Chiara always settled his mind. Truth was, just the sound of her steady voice always saw him through a rough patch. Thank God he'd had time with her after Joseph and Mike left to work out the plan with her.

She trusted the plan and so did he. It was a good one even though it had many moving parts. He ticked them off silently. Tomorrow Chiara and Joseph take an early morning boat to Venice. At the same time, Abbot Vartan sends Father Samvel, the librarian, to Vincenza.

With the librarian away, the abbot and the conservator, Father Davit, move the codex from the library to the conservatory. They hide it in Tom's empty backpack. Afterwards they walk him to the pier and board a *vaporetto* bound for Santa Lucia station. At the station he links up with Chiara, who had their tickets for Göttingen.

If things went right, Father Samvel wouldn't discover the missing *Panarion* for several days. By then he'd have the codex in Germany, leaving the abbot and conservator to explain the missing book to the police and the librarian.

Shaking off Joseph was the only monkey wrench in the works.

The plan had simplicity. Good enough. Yet, for all its simplicity success hinged on things out of his control. What if Zimmer overvalued the debt Abbot Vartan owed him? What if the abbot backed out at the last minute? He was after all allowing Tom to steal a national treasure. What if Father Samvel, the librarian, returned early, discovered the theft, and set the police on them before they crossed the border?

Dammit to hell! Shut down these sideways thoughts. You could only control the things you'd given to yourself and Chiara. The rest you had to trust to Zimmer, Vartan, and Davit.

Tom reached over Joseph's lap and gave Chiara's hand a tight squeeze. She returned the grip, stroking his palm with her index finger.

It was nearly dark when the steamboat tied up at the monastery pier. The motorman whipped his lines across the bow and stern, dropping them neatly over the cleats. With a calico cat slung under one arm, he used his free hand to ease his passengers over the gunnel and onto the deck. He handed the backpacks to Tom and a leather suitcase to Joseph. He winked at Tom. "This one feels pretty empty."

"Bringing toys home for our daughter." He knew the boatman meant no harm. Still, he felt naked and discovered, and the terrible urgency of the moment hit home.

On the pier, they huddled together against a raw wind that splashed whitecaps against the pilings and over the deck planks. Chiara's lips turned blue with cold. Tom draped an arm around her waist, drawing her closer. He felt her body quaver. Poor gal. Dark ridges circled her bright eyes. She'd not slept well since the dinner with Mike and Joseph. A flickering lantern at the monastery gate and a silhouette caught his eye. He recognized the figure of Abbot Vartan, whose heavy winter robes flew like stage curtains around his ankles. "Abbot Vartan's on his way," he told Chiara. They both shouted Hello and waved at the monk.

Joseph asked, "Who's that?"

Chiara dropped a hand on his sleeve. "That's our host, the abbot of the monastery."

"Good timing," Joseph said, stamping his boots on the deck. "Fearsome cold. Still, nuttin' like Milwaukee in January. Cain't figger why you kids pick an ice-box of an island for a little weekend sugar." He pulled his own jacket tighter around his shoulders.

Tom said, "I have unfinished business in the monastery. Best we could do for a little adult time. Hey!

Here's Abbot Vartan." He and Chiara flung their arms around the monk, nearly knocking the man over. Chiara kissed the abbot on both checks before introducing Joseph.

"Please ta meet ya," Joseph said.

"We are glad that God brought you to us, Joseph, and pray blessings on your stay," the abbot said. "Now let's hurry to the refectory. Dinner is served. You must be hungry. Our guest master will fetch your luggage."

A quarter hour later, the abbot settled the guests at his dinner table, introducing them to Father Samvel and the other monks. Tom started when he saw the empty seat where Father Davit, the conservator, usually sat. "Is Father Davit not joining us for dinner?" he asked the abbot. "I plan to talk with him tonight about the *Panarion*."

"Since yesterday he works and takes his meals in the conservatory," Father Samvel said. "He can prepare the *Panarion* for you if no one bothers him. Tomorrow morning he promises to meet us at the conservatory."

A whiff of garlic and basil and a clomp of heavy sandals turned their heads. "Food," Tom said, wheeling around for a closer look at the platter of shrimp and octopus. "Things look brighter already." He slid the toe of his shoe up and down Chiara's ankle. "We're alone tonight," he whispered. "No Faith."

When the chapel bell rang for Evensong, the abbot stood up and pulled Tom and Chiara aside. "As planned," he said, "Father Samvel leaves tomorrow for Vincenza. Father Davit and I will meet you at 10:30 a.m. in front of the conservatory. Do you remember the way?"

The next morning, Tom, Chiara, and Joseph ate breakfast at an empty table. Neither Abbot Vartan nor Father Davit nor Father Samvel were anywhere in sight. That Father Samvel did not eat breakfast made sense. He was already on his way to Vincenza on monastery business. But the other two? Tom ran an agitated hand through his hair. With Joseph at the table there was no chance to talk to Chiara.

The tower bell chimed eight times. "Time to go," Tom said. He looked around for Joseph. "Where in damnation is the big guy? You're late for the *vaporetto* pickup at the pier."

"Forgot his money belt and ran back to his room. He'll be back in five."

"Know your lines?" he asked Chiara.

"Don't worry about me, kid. Remember, acting runs in my blood. I can fake a bomb of a migraine."

"Your dad'd be proud of you. Still, tell me one more time what goes down when you reach Venice."

"So I tramp around the city with Joseph till noon, then I feign a migraine and tell Joseph to finish touring the sites without me. As soon as I lose him, I head for the train station. Meet you at 1:00 p.m. Right?"

"Perfect."

"Look, don't forget to bring my backpack with you. Got all my makeup and shampoo in it."

"I won't. Joseph is damned clingy these days. You may have trouble shaking him off."

"Nah. I'll do fine. I'll figure out how to pack him off on an errand. Besides he's probably choking with boredom, hanging out with us two lovebirds."

"Now remember, if I don't show up at the station by 3:00 p.m.—."

"I know, I know, darling," Chiara said, smiling an assurance. "That means there's a glitch in the plan, and I return to the monastery." Chiara cupped her hands around Tom's face and kissed him on the nose. "Nothing will go wrong. We've got it cold. I love you. Here's Joseph."

Chapter Thirty

Venice, February 1967

Tom saw Chiara and Joseph off at the pier then sprinted for the conservatory. As he rounded a corner to the building, he heard angry voices and skidded to a stop. He poked his head around the building. Oh my God! The abbot and another monk with his back turned to Tom were going at it hard. The abbot stamped a boot on the ground and poked the other monk in the chest with a finger. "We meet Tom in a few minutes. You must confess your treachery to him, just like you did to me last night."

My God, the abbot was speaking to Father Samvel, the librarian. Tom's lungs, already heaving from the run, nearly exploded. Son of a bitch. Samvel should be in Vincenza.

"On my most solemn vow," Father Samvel said, his words tumbling out, "I did only what blood ties require. How could I refuse?" His whimpers grew into loud, heaving sobs. "Father Davit is a cousin of my mother. He pleaded with me to say he worked around the clock in the conservatory, repairing the moldy binding on the *Panarion*.

"And yet you knew that was a lie," the abbot roared in the man's face.

"I can only plead remorse. Within minutes of his leaving yesterday, I turned desperate with guilt and called the police to look for Father Davit."

"But you did not inform me of this plan," Father Vartan scolded. "So now Father Davit has run away. And you bring the police into our affairs? What were you thinking, man?" The abbot seized the librarian by his robe and shook him violently. "You have much to answer for. My only consolation is that even without Father Davit present Tom can work with the codex."

"But of course," Father Samvel said. He turned away from the abbot, tears running down his cheeks and beading the cowl of his robe.

Tom coughed and stepped from behind the building. "Sorry, I'm a little late."

"Oh my God, Tom. You have heard?" the abbot said.

Tom nodded and stepped up to the monks. "I heard." He looked at Father Samvel. "I guess I know why you're not in Vincenza." There was a steely-edged anger in his voice. He turned to the abbot. "So, Father Davit left the monastery with the help of Father Samvel?"

The abbot gestured helplessly with his hands. "It seems so."

Tom pulled on the abbot's robe and drew him aside. His so-called simple plan had just tied itself up in knots, and now he had to get his hands on the *Panarion* with Father Samvel still on the monastery grounds. He wasn't sure what to do if the abbot had a change of heart and didn't play a true game.

"Father Vartan," Tom said, "I want you to take me to the conservatory. Right now. I need to make sure the *Panarion* is there. This can't wait."

"Of course," the abbot said. "Father Samvel, please let us into the conservatory."

The librarian jingled a ring of keys in his hand and picked one with a long shank and double bit. The lock didn't release. "I know another way in," he said. "Follow me, please." With the librarian leading the way, they crossed the winter lawn of the quadrangle and stopped at the far end of the portico. "It is but an unimportant passageway," the librarian said. "And very rarely opened. In former times, the doge used it as a dormitory for the more advanced cases of leprosy."

When they reached the entrance, Father Samvel turned the lock and admitted Tom and the abbot. Inside, he clicked a wall switch and a string of dim bulbs lit up a narrow staircase. "Follow me," he said, "and hold the rail." At the foot of the stairs, they found a cavernous passageway lined with rotting bed frames and doorless cupboards.

The passageway ended at a bolted iron gate that creaked open after Father Samvel turned a lock and kicked the foot plate with his boot. Inside the workshop a single desk lamp flickered. There was otherwise no sign that anyone had entered the room for days. Dust lay thick on the floor. Dirty coffee cups and bits and scraps of bread and cheese covered one worktable. A stack of letters waited on a desk to be opened.

Tom said, "Father Davit knew I was coming to work

on the *Panarion*. If he did what he promised, then he stored it in the wall safe at the other end of the workroom." He pointed to a robust metal door set high above a worktable. "I think we'll find the codex inside."

Tom wished he felt as sure as he sounded. Even if he got his hands on the *Panarion* that morning, he still had to lose Father Samvel, smuggle the book into his backpack, and meet Chiara at the train station. He prayed she made good on her promise to ditch Joseph. Well, solve one problem at a time. The rest will fall into place. He was not so sure.

The three men crossed the room, working their way around benches heaped with rolls of rag pulp, cylinders of beeswax, and spools of binder threads. Father Samvel hiked his robes and climbed on the table underneath the wall safe. Steadying himself with one hand, he inserted a long key into the lock, twisting it first to the right then to the left. When the door swung open, he poked a flashlight inside, pulling out binders, account books, and an old pair of shoes.

"Dear Mother of God. This is impossible." Father Samvel groaned like a wounded animal. He turned to Tom and the abbot. His Adam's apple bobbed up and down and his lips worked without making a sound. "The *Panarion*'s gone. Tom, help me down from this table." Tom reached for the librarian's outstretched hand and saw the monk safely to the floor.

"One minute, please," Tom said, grabbing the flashlight and climbing on the table "Goddammit," he said under this breath a moment later. "Not here. We need to check the library. Maybe Father Davit—."

"I'm sorry, Tom. I have no time just now," the abbot said, checking his wristwatch. "I will send one of the other monks to check in the library."

"No time?"

"No time. Father Samvel called the police last night. They arrive in moments. We meet them at the pier. Please follow me, Tom. We must hurry."

Tom grabbed a rubber mallet from a tabletop and flung it at a brick wall, his frustration spilling out in a string of fiery curses. In all his checking and double-checking of the plan, it never dawned on him that Father Davit was the one loose thread he'd forgotten. Of all the monks he'd met he trusted the conservator and antiquarian the most. Wrong again.

Tom barreled ahead of the two monks through the tunnel, crossing the quadrangle to the pier. A police launch rocked in the waves against the pilings. He counted five men onboard. Four wore the black capes and red lapels of the *Carabinieri,* the national police.

A thick overcoat, muffler, and hat covered a fifth man, who motioned to the policemen to disembark on the pier. "I am Sergio Pascali," he said, "senior investigator with the Special Branch of the Italian Ministry of Justice."

"I am Abbot Vartan. May I introduce our librarian, Father Samvel? And this is our American guest, Tom Weathering. Please follow me to my office."

A quarter hour later, settled on a sofa in the abbot's office next to Father Samvel, Tom's mind churned with one dark thought after another. National police. Missing

Panarion. Joseph shadowing Chiara. Speaking of Chiara, it was nearly noon. Had she ditched Joseph and made her way to the train station? The thought of Joseph giving her a hard time made his blood boil. No, scratch that worry. Chiara never met a man she couldn't handle. He, on the other hand, was about to meet a policeman whom he had no idea how to handle.

The abbot sat at his desk, absently drawing finger circles on a desk blotter. Tom thought he had never seen a man look so gloomy.

"I am sorry to bother your tranquility, Reverend Abbot," Pascali began. "You live here to escape the world, yet sometimes the world breaks in."

"Monastic life is never a simple thing. In fact—."

"I'm sure you're right, Reverend Abbot," Pascali said. "I have asked my men to wait in the hallway. To prevent any...disturbances. May I sit? I'll keep my coat on. I suffered a chill on the water." Father Samvel jumped up and brought a chair. Pascali fumbled in a coat pocket before pulling out a small notebook. He flipped over several pages. "Ah, yes. Yesterday Father Samvel called the police with a report of a missing monk, a certain Father Davit."

"That is so," the abbot said. "Without my knowledge."

"My business is to inform you of a possible crime. Maybe more than one."

"Please go on," the abbot said, his voice steady. "You may speak freely."

"After Father Samvel called us, we sent out a missing person's bulletin." Pascali flipped two more pages in his notebook. "Last night one of our officers found a monk's robes and sandals tied up in a sack and floating in the Grand Canal." The policeman consulted his notes again. "Ah yes. We also found in the bag a wet but readable receipt for a smart suit of clothes, more or less the size of your missing monk."

"No, it cannot be," cried the abbot, clapping a hand over his heart. "How do you know the robe and sandals belong to one of our men? There are many monasteries in Venice. God help us!"

"The owner stitched a name into the hem: Davit."

Tom's jaw dropped. The abbot and the librarian exchanged a horrified look, crossing themselves and mumbling a short prayer in Armenian.

Pascali said, "Perhaps not all is lost. Witnesses recall seeing a monk with a bulky package under his arm near the bookshops on the Venezia."

"Is it the bookshop that lies on the *Campiello del Tintor*?" Father Samvel asked.

"That's the one," Pascali said.

"It is well known to us," the abbot said. "The conservator visited it frequently to appraise the value of books for our insurance provider."

"Did you know," Pascal said, a mild sarcasm tinting his words, "that the man offered to sell one of your ancient books to the owners?"

"How do you know it is a book of our library?" Father Samvel asked.

"Venice requires its booksellers to inform the police when antiquities come up for sale," the policeman said.

"The bookseller confirmed that the volume in question was a very old codex, an Armenian translation of a writing by Saint Epiphanius."

"The *Panarion*," Tom groaned. "That's what brought me to the monastery and--."

Pascali raised a hand. "Later, young man, you will have time to give a statement." He flicked cigarette ash in his pant cuff.

The abbot, his face now nearly bloodless, said, "He would never trade in monastery property."

Tom couldn't hold back. "So, did he sell it?" he said, his fists jammed into his coat pockets, his mind splintering with anger at the unravelling of his plan.

"No, in fact he did not," Pascali said. "There is more."

God, what more could go wrong? Father Davit a missing person, the *Panarion* gone. How was he going to tell Chiara about this disaster? Or Zimmer? He glanced at Abbot Vartan, who sat silently, shoulders rounded, running his hands back and forth along the rounded edge of his desk.

"What more?" the abbot asked in a voice that sounded far away and tired.

"A shopkeeper saw a man in a smart suit and tie, together with a woman in a red coat, leaving that very shop. He carried a very large, wrapped package. We think the man was the monk Davit. Furthermore, we believe the package may have held your missing *Panarion*. Then there is this."

Tom braced himself. God. What more could go wrong he'd just asked himself. He was about to find out.

"A photographer named Moratori," the policeman said, "snapped a shot of the couple boarding a skiff tied up on the *Rio de San Giovanni Laterno*. Thought they were newly married and would want a photo. Turns out they did. But he had another backup shot. Thank goodness. We have that photo." He showed it to the abbot and Tom.

"Could be Mira Borja," Tom said. "Hard to tell in the light." No, by God, it was Mira. She'd outfoxed him again. He'd like nothing more than to throttle the damned librarian for his treachery.

Pascali folded his notebook and tucked it into a pocket. "They left the dock and motored in the direction of the Grand Canal. We still search for the lady in red and your monk in the fancy suit. And for the little boat." Pascal shrugged his shoulders and held out his hands, palms up. "I regret the news I bring. Now I return to the city. The four officers remain to take statements from the monks."

The phone on the abbot's desk rang. "Abbot Vartan speaking. Yes, this is the monastery of San Lazaro. You are looking for whom? Tom Weathering? Yes, in fact he's right here, professor. One moment." The abbot handed the receiver to Tom. "It's Professor Zimmer."

"Hello," Tom said, mildly alarmed at the unexpected call. "Is everything OK?" No. I'm not alone." The abbot nodded and ushered everyone from the office. For the longest minute of his life Tom listened and said nothing. When he hung up, he called to the abbot and met him at the door. His every muscle trembled like a newborn baby. There was no color in his face. In a voice low and somber he said, "I need to get to the train station and collect Chiara.

We can't stay here a moment longer."
"What has happened, my son?" the abbot asked.
"Mutti and Faith have disappeared."

(To Be Continued)

About The Author

Robert Hodgson lives in mid-Missouri with his wife Mary Timothy and their green-eyed Maltipoo "Irish." With their children and grandchildren, they enjoy sailing, traveling, cooking, and camping. Apart from writing fiction, Bob oil paints and gardens. A former professor of New Testament Literature at Missouri State University, he also spent nearly three decades as a staff member and consultant to American Bible Society. He holds a doctorate in Protestant theology from Heidelberg University in Germany, the first Roman Catholic to do so since the Reformation.

Afterword

Two actual writings from early Christianity sparked the idea for this novel. The one is a now lost letter of Apostle Paul to the Christians in the Asia Minor city of Laodicea. In this novel I also call the letter the "Androgyne Papyrus."

The other is the *Panarion*, Bishop Epiphanius' fourth-century AD catalog of heresies. Together the letter and the heresy book gave me a scaffold upon which I could hang my tale.

Epiphanius put together his book in the mid-fourth century AD. Libraries still stock modern editions. Paul's letter, written in the 50s AD, went happily lost. I say "happily" with tongue in cheek. After all, who wants to lose a book of the Bible?

The letter stems from a time when Paul started churches in western Asia Minor: Philippi, Colossae, Ephesus, and Laodicea. The New Testament includes writings to the first three of these early Christian communities.

We know about the missing Laodicean letter because Paul points to it in Colossians 4:13-16: "For I testify for him that he has worked hard for you and for those in Laodicea and in Hierapolis. Luke the beloved physician, and Demas greet you. Give my greetings to the brothers and sisters in Laodicea, and to Nympha and the church in her house. And when this letter has been read among you, have it read also in the church of the Laodiceans; and see that you read also the letter from Laodicea." (New Revised Standard Version).

The Laodicean community also shows up in the New Testament among the seven churches of Revelation: 3:14-22. "And to the angel of the church in Laodicea write: The words of the Amen, the faithful and true witness, the origin of God's creation. I know your works: you are neither cold nor hot...." (New Revised Standard Version).

Robert Hodgson, Jr.

Although only two New Testament passages mention the Christians in Laodicea we can guess at its social setting. Like other early congregations, it probably gathered in house churches or private homes.

If the sociology of the Laodicean church resembled the sociology of other early Christian communities, then it likely comprised day laborers, shopkeepers, farmers, veterans, even wandering charismatic evangelists. Slaves and citizens worshipped together in such a fellowship.

In a staggering piece of good luck, Colossians names the woman who owned the house in which the Laodiceans met. The letter calls her Nympha. I like to think of her as the leader of her house church.

If you want to dig deeper into these topics, I suggest the following titles:

Hedrick, Charles W. and Robert Hodgson, Jr., eds., *Nag Hammadi, Gnosticism, and Early Christianity.* Wipf and Stock, *2005.*

Platt, Rutherford H., *Lost Books of the Bible and Forgotten Books of Eden,* Apocryphile Press, 2005.

Robinson, James M., General editor, *The Nag Hammadi Library: A Translation of the Gnostic Scriptures.* Harper Collins, 1981.

Theissen, Gerd, *The First Followers of Jesus.* Translated by John Bowden. SCM Press, 1978.

Vermes, Geza, *The Complete Dead Sea Scrolls in English.* Penguin. 2012.

Williams, Frank, translator. *The Panarion of Epiphanius of Salamis. Book One.* 2nd edition. Brill, 2008. Nag Hammadi and Manichaean Studies 63.

Acknowledgements

First, I thank my family who supported and encouraged me during the writing of The Androgyne Papyrus. My wife Mary Timothy read drafts, helped kick ideas around, and kept the coffee pot on. She inspired the character of Chiara O'Keeffe. Jennifer Hodgson McGee designed the cover. Sigrid, Kate, and Robert Hodgson III coached me into the world of online publishing. Mary Hodgson Phillips, Brian Treece, and Price Phillips along with David, Ema Blue, and Jonathan McGee cheered me on from early days.

About halfway through a third draft, Nancy Burdick, Millie Henry, and Lisa Aguilar kindly invited me into their writing circle. For nearly four years they walked with me through the story, ensuring that I wrote what I meant and meant what I wrote. I remain in awe at their mastery of writerly craft.

I want to thank Keija Parsinnen and Gordon Sauer, along with other members of the Quarry Heights Writers Group, for their help with early chapters. To Charles Houser, retired senior editor at American Bible Society, I'm indebted. He believed in the book and gave solid guidance.

I also am grateful to Charles W. Hedrick, my learned friend and former colleague at Missouri State University. He read the final draft with a critical eye. For historical and technical advice on the Vietnam era I owe thanks to my cousin Larry Wyman. A veteran of that conflict, he helped me write honestly and truly about a soldier's life.

Sharon Laborde edited, formatted, and uploaded the book on Kindle Direct Publishing. For the professionalism she showed in these pre-production steps I owe her a hearty thank you.

Made in the USA
Columbia, SC
08 November 2022

70667755R00139